DREAMRIDER

DREAMRIDER

BARRY JONSBERG

Alfred A. Knopf
New York

THIS IS A BORZOI BOOK PUBLISHED BY ALFRED A. KNOPF

Copyright © 2006 by Barry Jonsberg

Published in the United States by Alfred A. Knopf, an imprint of Random House Children's Books, a division of Random House, Inc., New York.
Originally published in Australia by Allen & Unwin in 2006.

KNOPF, BORZOI BOOKS, and the colophon are registered trademarks of Random House, Inc.

www.randomhouse.com/teens

Educators and librarians, for a variety of teaching tools, visit us at
www.randomhouse.com/teachers

Library of Congress Cataloging-in-Publication Data
Jonsberg, Barry.
Dreamrider / Barry Jonsberg. — 1st American ed.
   p. cm.
Originally published in Australia by Allen & Unwin in 2006.
Summary: Harangued by his father about his weight and bullied in all the many schools he has attended, teenaged Michael finds some comfort in his ability to experience "lucid" dreaming but then starts to notice that the things that happen in his dreams are starting to occur in the real world as well.
ISBN 978-0-375-84457-7 (trade) — ISBN 978-0-375-94457-4 (lib. bdg.)
[1. Lucid dreams—Fiction. 2. Bullying—Fiction. 3. Overweight persons—Fiction. 4. Emotional problems—Fiction. 5. High schools—Fiction. 6. Schools—Fiction. 7. Australia—Fiction.] I. Title.
PZ7.J7426Dr 2008
[Fic]—dc22
2007028929

Printed in the United States of America

February 2008

10 9 8 7 6 5 4 3 2 1

First American Edition

For Brendan, Kari, Kris, and Lauren

DREAMRIDER

There is something wrong with the light. I'm not sure what. I'm not sure of anything.

I keep my eyes closed. It's easier. I focus on the pain in my leg and the pain in my arm.

Pain is simple.

Unlike everything else.

When I open my eyes, the light is a blade. I feel the sides of the bed. Hard, cold, burning. People move within the light, touching, talking, and then leaving. I don't trust them.

I'm sick. I don't know where I am. Why? is too big a question. So I close my eyes and hug the darkness with pain at its center. I am drowning in a sea of doubt. Memories are my lifeline. Images appear in the dark.

I remember . . .

Monday

1.

I killed two kids at school today.

My first day. I wandered the school grounds, looking for differences. The way the sun hit the grass, the arrangement of litter, the smells.

They came at me from opposite sides. I kept my head down. Part of me knew it would do no good, but I walked and watched from the edge of vision.

"Hey. You. Fat bastard."

On cue. Like a film you've seen before so you know the words before they're spoken. I walked. Kept my head down, looking for differences. I couldn't see any.

"I'm talking to you, fat bastard."

I stopped. But I kept my head down. Still.

A blade of grass. I watched. It differed. Maybe the way the spine curved, or the sheen of green. Wrong, somehow. An insect crawled along the blade's curve. It changed the world. Everything changes the world—the insect on the grass, the shadows over the oval.

They arrived. I heard their breathing. Their dark shadows slanted across the grass. I waited.

"I'm talking to you, fat boy. And when I'm talking to you, you should look at me."

"Yeah. Look at him, fat boy."

I looked at him. He had freckles. A face someone had doodled on, not getting the patches of color right. Dark red hair. Matted, as though he hadn't showered in a week. His eyes were light blue, the color of pale flowers in cold climates. I tried to see beyond them. I can do that. There was only pain, loneliness, and fear. There's always fear.

We stared at each other, the fat boy and the boy with ice for eyes.

And I waited.

"So what have you got to say for yourself, fat boy? Eh? Why'd you ignore me? Too good for me? Is that it, huh? He thinks he's too good for us, Damien."

Damien was small, thin and wiry. An athlete. His eyes were

screwed up. I couldn't read them because he was facing the sun. He stood like someone who owned the ground beneath him.

"Yeah, I reckon, Callum. Why do you think you're too good for us, fat boy?"

"I'm just a fat boy," I said. "That's all. I'm not too good for you. I'm not good enough. I'm fat. I'm nothing."

The red-haired boy was confused. It happens that way sometimes. They want the right to attack. But I was agreeing. If they bashed me now, they'd feel bad about themselves. And they wanted their punches to be pure. Righteous.

The red-haired boy shifted, put his hands on his hips.

"Are you being a wiseass, fat boy?"

"No," I said.

"Well, I think you are. What do you reckon, Damien? Is he a wiseass?"

"Yeah. He's a wiseass big-time. You're asking for it, fat bastard. So why don't you say you're sorry? Maybe if you apologize, we'll forget it this time."

The red-haired boy moved in a little.

"Yeah. We need an apology, fat boy."

"I'm sorry," I said.

Callum poked me in the chest with a hard finger.

"You need to *show* you're sorry. How about on your knees? Yeah, get on your knees and say you're sorry for being such a wiseass."

So I got down on my knees. In the middle of the oval. As though I was praying. I bent my head. The blade of grass was closer now and still wrong. I focused. The insect climbed its plane, the east face of a green mountain. I counted the legs. They seemed right. And then I saw the difference.

It was subtle. The way the light hit the stalk. The sun was behind me, and the boys' shadows pointed away, toward where it would set. But the light on this blade of grass came from the wrong direction. The right side of the blade was polished, burnished by light, and the left shadowed. Wrong. The tip of the blade, curved away from me, should have been touched by gold.

I knew. So I stood.

"I told you to get on your knees, fat boy," said Callum.

I looked at him closely. Once I notice the first difference, even if it's small, others follow, bigger and bigger, until the whole world is different. Callum's eyes were brown now. His freckles shifted into a birthmark on his right cheek. His hair was a darker shade of red. Like rust.

I could take my time, so I turned to Damien. He had shrunk and the athlete was gone. He no longer squinted into the sun, because the sun had moved directly above us. I wanted it that way.

"I'm not sorry," I said. "I haven't done anything to be sorry about. You started this. Not me. So I'm not sorry, and I'm not getting down on my knees."

Callum glanced at his mate. My words were a detour into unfamiliar territory, and he had no map to give directions. I wanted him to bluster. So he did.

"I don't care what you think, fat boy," he said. "I don't give a shit. So you'd better say sorry real quick or . . ."

"I'll be sorry?" I said.

"Yeah," he said.

"Look," I said. "I'll tell you what I think and you'll listen. Every school I've been to, you were there. Sometimes you were taller, sometimes smaller. Your hair changes, your clothes change, but you don't. Not what's inside. It's always dark. I can taste it, that darkness. And it tastes of blood and fear and hopelessness."

"You're weird," said Damien.

"It's time to hit me," I said.

The boys glanced at each other. Nervous. Callum's eyes shifted back to me. One had turned green. His fist balled and he rocked back on his heels to get the weight right. He was scared but he had to punch me now. I'd given him no choice.

His fist swung back, and I put my face forward a little. I watched as the knuckles arced toward me. It was not a bad punch, considering I had chipped his confidence. I'd felt worse. When his fist landed on my cheek, just below my left eye, I felt the bone give. But I didn't fall.

Callum stepped back and rubbed his hand. Blood snailed down the side of my face. I smiled.

"Is that the best you can do?" I said. "Come on, guys. How about the two of you, eh? Here."

I turned slightly to present them with equal target areas. I opened my legs for balance and put my hands behind my back.

"Let's go," I said. "I haven't got all day."

I kept the sun above me as they punched and kicked. At one point my nose exploded, sending a plume of blood in the air. The droplets glittered and flecked Callum's cheek. I lost some teeth to another blow. I felt them splinter. I spat the pieces into Damien's face and smiled.

They stopped then. They stood panting, faces bloodied. I wouldn't let them run, though they wanted to. I was the most terrifying thing they had ever seen. The broken bones, the blood, the smashed teeth. But the greatest horror was my smile.

"I'm a little disappointed, boys," I said. I rolled my bruised tongue around and discovered a couple more shattered teeth. I spat the pieces into my hand and held them out to Callum. He reached out and I placed them into his palm.

"Here's what I think," I continued. "You should apologize to me. I mean, look. I'm a mess and I didn't deserve it. The least you can do is say you're sorry."

"Sorry," said Damien.

"Sorry," said Callum.

"On your knees," I said.

They started crying then and I allowed that. As they knelt before me, I noticed spreading stains on the front of their shorts.

That made me angry. I thought they were more scared than sorry. They were mourning the outcome, not the events before it.

"Get up," I said.

They did, of course. They stood before me, heads bowed. Crushed.

"You're not sorry enough," I said. "So I'm going to have to make you sorry enough."

I made the sun move and circle. It created a strange effect, the shadows dancing over our bodies. Darkness dappled the grass and washed us. I must have looked more terrifying then, as shadows swirled. My face—my crushed nose, my broken teeth, my bloodied eye sockets—plunged into darkness briefly, before the grisly mess lit up again. Demonic.

I lifted my arms, and the heads of the boys rose, as if connected by a thread to my outstretched fingers. They knew something terrible was going to happen. I let them bathe in the coldness of knowledge while I kept their eyes on the flashing ruin of my face.

I lifted my arms out and above my shoulders. And then I swept down and inward. I braced my fingers and thrust my hands beneath their ribs. I felt the warm slide into their bodies, flesh parting like water. I fixed attention on their eyes, flooded with dull surprise. I kept my hands still for a moment and then pushed up and in, until I found the slimy knots of muscle, the pulse of blood pumping, jerking. I pulled back down.

The boys stood for a moment, but their eyes were snuffed.

They crumpled onto the stained grass. I let the sun revolve once more as I stood above their bodies; then I raised my head and howled my dark joy at the sky.

I knew the glass would be behind me. If I turned—when I turned—I would see the slight curve in its surface and my own young face, a ghostly reflection. There would be nothing behind the glass, but I would sense movement within the blackness at its center. Then the colors flickering into life. A burst of orange in the top right corner, a streak of yellow. Finally, the tight ball of terror as something stirred beneath the surface. Air hot, pain in my chest, a scream frozen on my lips.

I would face that. Later. I spread my bloodied arms and held the world. I'm the fat boy. I'm Michael Terny.

I killed two kids at school today.

2.

I stood under the shower without moving. I can do that for an hour sometimes. Just letting the water flow over me. Safe. I didn't have time today, though.

First day of school and the eggs were in the microwave.

I toweled myself dry and thought about clothes. Clothes can make a difference. Not always. Not often, I had to admit. I chose blue shorts. Not too nerdy. Plain white T-shirt. Scuffed runners. I examined my image in the wardrobe mirror, but not for long.

As I went into the kitchen, Dad brushed past and into the bathroom. He wasn't in a good mood. The microwave pinged and I shoved bread into the toaster. Mary stood by the back door. She smiled as I opened the fridge.

"Sleep well, Michael?" she asked.

"Not bad," I lied.

"Nervous about your first day?"

"A bit."

The toast popped and I buttered two slices. Not mine. Low-fat spread on mine. Dad insisted.

"Ah, you'll be all right, mate," she said. "Just don't take any crap. Okay?"

I nodded, took the eggs from the microwave, and put the bowl on the table. Mary came over and lowered her voice.

"Your lunch is in your bag, Michael. And I think a little extra something might have fallen in. By accident." She gave me a slow wink and I had to smile.

"Thanks," I said. She did that for me sometimes. A bag of chips, a chocolate biscuit. It was our secret. Dad would lose it if he knew. I was never allowed to eat from school canteens. He didn't trust me with food. Trouble often happened at lunchtime, when I was sitting on a bench by myself with low-fat yogurt, crackers, fruit spread out around me. Someone would say something. Someone eating a cheeseburger.

"What's that shit, fat boy?" he'd say. And then I'd have to pretend I hadn't heard. And then . . .

I spooned scrambled eggs from the bowl onto my toast as Dad came in, hair slicked back, wearing an undershirt and flip-flops. It was his first day too. He sat opposite me and glanced at my plate, checking out the portion. He always did that. He rationed everything. Then he helped himself to eggs. Mary sat beside him, but she wasn't eating. She didn't do breakfast.

"Ah," she said. "The men off to work. Warms my heart, so it does."

Dad just shoveled egg into his mouth. Mary watched us and smiled.

"You can't work without a decent breakfast," she said. "You need to keep your blood sugars up. The pair of you. Stops you flagging during the day."

"I'm still hungry," I said. That was a mistake. "A bit," I added.

Dad pointed his fork at me.

"You're always hungry, you," he said. "If you spent less time feeding your face and more time exercising, you wouldn't be in that bloody state."

Mary sighed.

"Now, Joe," she said. "Come on. Everyone needs a solid breakfast. It's the most important meal of the day."

I thought this was a bit rich, coming from someone who never seemed to eat.

Dad didn't reply. He finished his meal in silence and glanced at his watch.

"I'll give you a lift to school," he said. "Only today, though."

I was pleased. I hate that first bus journey to a new school.

You can never get a seat. Even if there are plenty of empty seats, they are always being saved for a friend. Even the empty rows turn out to be reserved. And then you have to get up while everyone stares at you.

Mary kissed me on the cheek as I left.

"Have a good day, Mikey," she whispered as I closed the front door.

Dad started up the truck and we set off, belching a black cloud of diesel behind us. The truck had seen better days, but the engine turned over and it got us from A to B. Dad said that was the important thing.

I watched the town roll past. Dad's not great on small talk, and I didn't have anything to say. I was hoping the school would be in a decent neighborhood. That can be important. If you're in a good area, then the kids are less likely to cause trouble, in and out of class. Not always, though. Some of the worst trouble I've had has been in "good" middle-class schools. I hadn't seen my new school yet. Dad had arranged it all. Talked to the principal, filled out the enrollment forms. Didn't mention it to me. Mary didn't know much either when I asked her. Like I said, Dad wasn't good at communication, and I didn't push him.

We drove through slowly changing suburbs where the houses were more run-down. Some of the shops had boards on the windows. Cars were older, gardens less cared for. And then we pulled out on a main road, and I could see the school in the distance. It had to be.

I knew at once I wasn't going to like it. The buildings looked clean, but they were too close together, jammed in and uncomfortable. Kids were milling outside, getting out of cars or walking from the bus stop. I couldn't tell anything about the school from them. Kids are the same everywhere. But at least they knew each other. I knew no one.

Dad pulled into the bus bay.

"Stay out of trouble, okay?" he said.

There was no point telling him I didn't have much choice, that trouble found me. He saw things differently.

"Okay," I said.

"And check out the sports. See if they've got a boxing club."

I nodded. He said this at every school. None of them ever had a boxing club. I'd given up telling him.

I got out and he drove off without another word.

I hate that first time, standing across the road from a school and knowing you've got to go in, sort things out, talk to people, attend classes with strangers staring at you. I had done it many times, but I still hated it. I crossed the road quickly and went in through the gates.

I wanted to get inside the building, but they hadn't opened the doors. I was forced to wait on the expanse of concrete outside the main entrance, an island among continents of surging kids. I kept my head down and tried to be invisible.

"Hey."

I shifted the schoolbag on my shoulder and glanced up,

without moving my head. The voice was light and friendly, but that doesn't always mean safe.

She was small and rounded, with dark hair that swung across her eyes. I took in the basic details and looked down again. Her eyes, beneath the curtain of hair, were kind. I always notice the eyes first.

"New kid?"

"Yeah," I mumbled. I shifted the straps on my schoolbag again.

"Can I help?"

I shrugged.

"Have you got a schedule?"

I shook my head.

"Well, that's the first thing you need to get sorted. Go to the office. They'll help."

"Thanks," I said to the floor.

"No worries. See you round, maybe."

"Yeah. Thanks," I added, but she had gone. A friendly kid. I was grateful for that. And sorry I hadn't been more friendly in return.

The bell sounded. It was harsh and cold. Kids flooded toward various entrances. I moved as well. If you want to be invisible, it's good to move with the crowds.

I suppose I wasn't looking where I was going. Too focused on the door and not paying enough attention. I caught the boy with my shoulder, knocking his drink carton. A spurt of iced coffee landed on his arm even though he arched his body away.

"Sorry," I mumbled.

He didn't reply. He just glared at me, pale blue eyes below a fringe of tangled red hair. I thought briefly of offering to buy him another drink, but I decided it wasn't wise.

"Sorry," I repeated, and turned away toward the steps. I could feel his eyes on my back.

It was dark inside the school, and there was a musty smell of old papers. At least the signs on the walls were clear, and I found my way to the office quickly. A woman took my name, and I sat in the waiting area. Kids wandered through the office, collecting schedules, checking in skateboards. One or two glanced at me, but I looked the other way. After about five minutes, another woman came out from an office down the corridor and called my name. I followed her. She sat behind a desk, and I sat in a soft chair facing her. She tapped on a keyboard and then smiled at me.

"Welcome to Millways High School, Michael. I'm Miss Palmer and I'm the assistant principal in charge of curriculum. We hope you're going to be happy here."

"Thanks, miss," I said.

She had kind eyes, like the girl outside. Two people promising kindness. That didn't happen often on the first day. It offered a balance to the bad feelings that seemed soaked into the school building. Her eyes were brown and soft, with a tinge of severity beneath the surface, as if her mood could switch quickly. Her hair was gray and coarse, tied back from her face and clipped at the nape of her neck. It made her appear stern. Maybe that was the idea. I took in all this in one sideways glance.

I'm good at details. I suppose it's because I keep looking for differences. It makes you pay attention.

"Now, your father has already done the paperwork for your enrollment, Michael, so I just have to give you your schedule and take you to Home Group. Your Home Group teacher is Mr. Atkins. You'll like him. He's the person who arranges everything for you, does all the administration. And he's the person you would go to if you were experiencing any problems. Social as well as academic. So, he's your closest contact at the school, at least among the teaching staff. Do you understand?"

I nodded. Miss Palmer took a sheet from the printer beside her computer and handed it to me.

"Here's your schedule," she said. "You'll soon get used to the place. Anywhere new seems strange at first, but it won't take you long to settle down, I'm sure."

She leaned back in her chair. There was something else she wanted to say, but she didn't know how to tackle it. I waited.

"Now, Michael . . . or do you prefer Mike?"

"Michael."

"Well, Michael, I've not yet received reports from your previous schools, but your father told me you had been to several in the last few years. Can you remember how many?"

I shrugged. "Seven."

"Seven! In, what . . ." She glanced down at the enrollment form. "Less than four years?" She smiled. "I guess you don't need me to tell you about coming to terms with strange places. You must be quite the expert. But your father also said you've had bad experiences in the past. Some bullying." She tapped her front teeth with a pen. "Can you tell me anything about that?"

I shrugged and studied a poster over her right shoulder. I was starting to like Miss Palmer. She seemed honest, and that hadn't been the case in my other schools. Bullying was something they wanted to keep buried. Maybe Miss Palmer didn't see it like that. I wasn't sure it would change anything, but that was beside the point.

There was a silence for a few moments. Miss Palmer looked me over. She was deciding whether to bring up the subject of my weight. I was interested to see if she had the courage.

"Michael, I wish I could give a guarantee you won't be bullied here, but we both know I can't do that. Kids are, I'm afraid, pretty much the same wherever you go, and some are not very tolerant of . . . differences. What I *can* say is, the school won't tolerate bullying of any kind. We take the matter very seriously. However, we can't do much if we don't know it's happening. I want you to promise, Michael, that you will report straight to me if you have a problem, and I'll nip it in the bud. Do you promise?"

"Yes, miss," I said, though it was a lie. It wasn't as easy as that. Miss Palmer knew it too. I could tell from her eyes.

"Okay," she said. "Well, let's hope it's not necessary. Most of the kids here are decent. But there is a minority. . . . Anyway, time to take you to Home Group."

I picked up my bag and followed her down the corridor. We walked through a courtyard with a patch of grass and a few benches scattered around. The windows of the building crowded me. I felt I was being watched. Everywhere was silent. I tried to fix the scene in my mind. I do that all the time. It helps when I'm spotting differences. It's become a habit.

We went up a flight of stairs and along another corridor. The inside of the school was in a bad state. The walls hadn't been painted in years, and there were cracks in the tiles. Classroom doors were scuffed and paint was peeling. There was a smell of dampness.

"This is A Block," said Miss Palmer. "The rooms are numbered according to the floor. This is the first floor, so the first number is always a one here. Mr. Atkins will give you a student diary, which has a map in it. You'll get used to it. Your Home Group is in A-fifteen. Here we are."

We stood outside the door for a moment. This was always the worst time, wondering what was on the other side. Then again, the first day was full of worst times. The first lesson, the first teacher, the first student you had to sit with, the first recess. I composed my face. There was nothing for it but to go in.

The footsteps were loud on the tiles. Miss Palmer and I turned at the same time. A boy was walking toward us. He had red hair and a damp patch on the sleeve of his T-shirt. I turned my eyes quickly back to the door of A15.

"Jamie Archer," said Miss Palmer. "Why aren't you in Home Group?"

"Had to clean my shirt, miss. Some Wrenbury spilled iced coffee over me."

"Just hurry, Jamie."

I could hear his footsteps down the corridor. I could feel his eyes on the back of my neck.

"Do you want me to come in and introduce you?" asked Miss Palmer.

I shrugged.

"No thanks, miss."

I knew that would only make it worse, like a kid being brought in by his mum. Miss Palmer seemed to understand.

"I'll leave you here, then," she said. "Have a good day, Michael. And remember what I said about bullying."

She started to walk off.

"Miss?" I said.

"Yes, Michael?"

"What's a Wrenbury?"

She pinched the top of her nose and closed her eyes.

"Wrenbury is a place, Michael. It's a local school for students with special needs."

I nodded. That made sense. There were sounds coming from behind the closed door, a quiet murmur of conversation, punctuated by a giggle or a shout. I waited until Miss Palmer had disappeared down the corridor, took a deep breath, and opened the door.

3.

It was as if I had flicked a switch. Everyone in the room went quiet, and sixteen or seventeen kids turned to stare at me.

I went red. I couldn't help it. It always happened, no matter how hard I fought. I stood in the doorway and tried to take in as much of the room as possible while keeping my head down. Eye contact didn't seem like a good idea.

The classroom was lit by a bank of windows along the far side of the room. Desks were arranged in groups, and the sun slanted across the back two. "I love dick" was written across the back of one chair in black pen. Most of the desks had graffiti on them, and plastic was peeling where kids had scraped metal rulers across the edges. The ceiling had strip lighting in panels, and a few were cracked. One light flickered. But it was a nice room. I liked it. The sun shining on the back wall gave it warmth. It was a place where someone could be happy.

To my right was a whiteboard. In front of that was a teacher's desk. Sitting behind the desk, marking a roll, was a teacher, Mr. Atkins presumably. He was chewing on a pen. He stood and came toward me. Mr. Atkins was tall, about fifty years old, with thinning gray hair. His eyes sparked with humor and friendliness. But I also noticed that the spark was only on the surface; I could read unhappiness beneath it.

"You must be Michael," he said, offering his hand.

I moved to take it, but at the last moment he withdrew and reached up toward my face. I took a half-step backward, but it was too late. He tapped my nose lightly and then withdrew his hand and opened it. In the palm lay a shining two-dollar coin. He grinned and a groan ran around the class.

"Take no notice of these cynics, Michael. They are world-weary and far too old for their tender years." He leaned toward me, as if to whisper a secret. "You and I know there is always, always room for wonder and that if we do not embrace the impossible, then the only thing we are left with is the plain and ugly world of the possible. How dull!"

He extended his hand again, the coin gold against the white of his palm. This time I took it, and he gave my hand a firm shake. There was no metal hardness as I pressed back. The coin had disappeared. Mr. Atkins winked at me.

"We've been expecting you. Welcome to Home Group Fifteen, the worst Home Group in the entire school, full of delinquents, losers, and the terminally dysfunctional. If you fall into this category, Michael, then you have found your spiritual home. If not . . . and if I am any judge, you are none of those things . . . then just sit back and enjoy the show."

He put his hand on my shoulder and turned to face the class.

"Losers and delinquents, may I introduce Michael, the new member of our Home Group. Now, if it wasn't bad enough that he drew the shortest of straws in getting allocated to us, Michael also suffers from knowing no one in the entire institution. Michael has come from interstate. Why? you might ask—and it would be a good question, since anyone who has been here for a few months understands that the rational thing is to head away from this place rather than toward it. Be that as it may, Michael is here, for good or ill, and we need to allocate him a mentor, someone to show him around, point out where the smokers go to get away from teachers, usher him in the direction of the culinary centerpiece of this wonderful place of learning, the canteen, and generally show him what's what. I need a volunteer. Lauren. Thank you very much."

The class hadn't moved, and there were certainly no volunteers, but I could see this was going to be Mr. Atkins's style. He sighed theatrically and led me toward a group of girls at the back. One of the girls had a small smile on her face. Her eyes told me she liked Mr. Atkins.

"Lauren, my dear," said Mr. Atkins. "You do understand that when I was referring to losers and delinquents, you were the exception to the rule, a shining light in the otherwise bleak assemblage of those who pass for students in this place. Lauren, meet Michael. Michael, this is Lauren Moss. One of Millways High School's finest. Lauren, take care of him. He seems a decent boy, and we don't want him corrupted too soon, now, do we? Michael, I leave you in Lauren's tender care."

Mr. Atkins winked at both of us and disappeared back to the front of the class. I shuffled from foot to foot while Lauren looked me up and down. She didn't seem impressed.

"So what do you need to know, Michael?" Lauren said. She said it pleasantly, but there was an edge to her voice, a hint of irritation. Even as she spoke, her gaze switched back to her friends.

"I dunno," I said. "I don't know what I need to know."

"Oh," said Lauren. She wasn't listening. Suddenly I made a decision. It was easier this way.

"I'll be okay," I said. "Go back to your friends, if you want."

"You sure?"

She didn't try to hide her eagerness.

"Yeah."

"I can meet you at recess, if you want. Show you around." She was attempting a trade-off so she'd feel better.

"Nah. I'll be all right."

"Well, if you're sure."

So she returned to her friends while I shuffled to a space at the back of the class and sat, gazing out the window. I didn't even notice when someone else approached from my right. A shadow fell and I glanced up.

It was the girl from outside. The girl with the kind eyes. I risked a closer look, darting my eyes between her face and the tiles on the floor. Her dark hair came to her jawline and then swept up and under. She was plump. Nothing like my size, of course, but definitely rounded. Her eyes were deep and brown, filled with kindness. It was all I could do not to stare at them. I glanced back at the floor, briefly taking in a nose that was slightly too wide and a mouth that turned down at the edges. She was not pretty, not really. But there was a warmth about her.

I took all this in quickly. I even risked checking out the classroom. The other students had returned to their conversations, but I could tell by their sidelong glances that they were weighing me up, so to speak. A couple of the boys were leaning in to each other and laughing.

The girl sat next to me and smiled.

"Hi, again. I'm Leah McIntyre. Pleased to meet you."

"Michael Terny."

She smiled at me for a moment, as if unsure what to say next.

"Phew. You're a big one, Michael," she said finally, but her eyes gave the true story. She wasn't being nasty. She was being honest. I liked that.

"Yeah," I said. "Fattest kid you've ever seen, probably."

"Yep," she said. "And I've seen a few. Not that I've got anything to shout about." She patted herself on the stomach. "A little too fond of the cakes." She laughed. "Well, it's more of a love affair, really."

I smiled. I knew exactly what she meant.

"Do you get shit about your weight?" she asked.

I shrugged.

"Hmm." She thought for a while. "Anyway, Fat Mick, let's see your schedule. I might be able to help you out."

"It's Michael," I said. "Fat Michael to you."

She grinned. I liked her. I didn't care that the other students were laughing at us.

When the bell went for first lesson, Mr. Atkins took me to the door. He gave me a student diary and a pat on the back.

"A small token of our esteem and respect," he said.

For some reason, as I walked down the corridor, I felt inside my pocket. My hand closed around a coin. I didn't need to take it out to know that it was a two-dollar coin. A gleaming two-dollar coin that hadn't been there before.

I had math first. I sat at the side of the class. If you sit at the front, you get marked as a nerd, and you can't sit at the back.

That's where the tough kids hang, and I didn't want to provoke anyone.

Some kids stared at me and whispered behind their hands. They didn't laugh out loud, but only because the teacher was strict and glared at anyone who made a noise. That suited me. English was next and that was okay as well. The teacher was friendly enough, but without much control over the class. A couple of the boys made snide comments, but she either didn't hear or decided to ignore them. Again, that was fine. Anything to avoid trouble.

At recess I wandered out to the oval. Leah had offered to meet me, but I'd said I would be fine. I didn't want her to feel obliged. She'd want to spend time with her friends, after all. Anyway, I needed to explore by myself. I had to find my place, and I could only do that alone. I always found a niche, at every school. Somewhere that felt right, where I could be by myself. It's difficult to describe, but I always knew it when I found it. In our new house, for example, it wasn't my bedroom; it was the steps outside the laundry. It felt good there. Quiet. I knew there would be a place like that somewhere on the school grounds. It was just a case of finding it.

I skirted groups of kids littering the oval and ignored their stares. There was a tree away from the main area, and I headed toward it. It was a hot day and I needed shade. Most of the other trees already had groups of kids under them. I sat under my tree and faced the oval. I didn't want it to seem like I was staring at anyone.

I opened my lunch bag and found the treat Mary had packed. It was a big slab of chocolate cake, already starting to melt in the heat. I picked up a piece, and it crumbled in my fingers. I had a chunk almost to my mouth when I stopped. I thought of Leah. She liked cake. Maybe it would be nice to save it for her. Then again, she might think I was hitting on her. It was a problem.

A shadow fell across my feet. I looked up. The shadow belonged to a boy. His eyes were brown. And hard.

"This place is out-of-bounds," he said.

"Is it?" I said. "I didn't know. I'm new."

"Yeah, I know. You think I wouldn't have noticed you before? You're a little difficult to miss, mate." He squatted down next to me. "You like cake, eh?"

I shrugged.

"Figures," he said. "So how many of those do you have a day? I mean, to get to your size, you must get through, what, five or six?"

I didn't say anything, but I looked around for differences. It's instinctive. I couldn't see any, though. The boy sighed.

"Listen, mate. When I ask a question, you answer. Is that clear?" His voice was calm, as if explaining something simple to someone of limited intelligence. There wasn't any anger or aggression in it. And that scared me.

"Yeah," I said.

"Anyway," he continued. "You must eat plenty. Do you know what I think?"

I didn't know if that was a question I was supposed to answer, but he carried on without pause.

"I think I would be doing you a favor if I took it off you. You know, one less cake a day. You might lose some weight. That would help, wouldn't it? Like, I'm your local Weight Watchers. What do you think?"

"You can have it," I said. I held out the cake. He seemed disgusted.

"I don't want to eat it," he said. "Not after it's been in your fingers. Have you never learned elementary hygiene, my fat friend? No, this is what I want to do with it."

He took the cake from me and smashed it into my face, rubbing it around my nose and up into my eyes, forcing it into my hair. I kept still.

"Look at me," he said.

I scraped cake away from my eyes. He was still squatting and his face was a blank. There wasn't any sign of enjoyment or the adrenaline rush I'd normally see. He wiped crumbs from his fingers onto my shirt.

"For some reason, mate, I've taken a dislike to you," he said. "I don't know why. It happens like that sometimes, doesn't it?" His voice was quiet and reasonable.

"Yeah," I said. I knew an answer was required.

"Anyway," he continued, "it goes without saying that this was merely an unfortunate accident. Nor will you mention this." He flicked out a hand, and it caught me across the nose. It wasn't hard. Not a punch, but it stung. Blood gathered in my nostrils and dripped down into the brown sticky mess on my top lip. "Because that didn't happen. I'm sure we understand each other." He sighed. "Well, I'd love to stay here chatting, but, like I said, this place is out-of-bounds, and I wouldn't want to get in trouble. I've a reputation to maintain. My name's Martin, by the way." He held out his hand. I took it and he gave me a firm handshake. "Pleased to meet you. And welcome to Millways High."

I sat in the corner, my head tilted back, an ice pack pressed to my nose. It didn't seem to be doing much good. I could feel a trickle of blood down my throat.

"What do you know about this, Jamie?" asked Miss Palmer.

I was glad I didn't have to look at him. The rage was clear in his voice, though.

"Nothin'," he said. "I told you. I had nothin' to do with it. Why are you always pickin' on me?"

"I'm not accusing you of anything, Jamie," said Miss Palmer. Her voice was calm and reasonable. I could feel the effort it took. "The fact is that when Mr. Atkins found Michael, you were with him. Laughing. I think it's reasonable to ask you what happened."

"I told you. He comes in from the oval, with that crap all over him. Yeah, I laughed. Who wouldn't? But it wasn't my fault."

"Michael?"

I shifted the ice pack a little.

"I tripped over the tree roots, miss. It was an accident."

"You see. You heard him. I had nothin' to do with it. There's two of us saying that. What does it take to make you believe me? I'm tired of this shit. . . ."

"Jamie, you can go. But a word of advice. Be very careful. Of your language, your attitude. Everything. Do you understand?"

He grunted. I heard him leave, his rage loud in the slap of his footsteps and the slamming of the door. I knew I'd have to face that rage eventually. That's the way it worked. I lowered my head and carefully removed the ice pack. It was stained red and chocolate brown. Mr. Atkins sat opposite me. He cupped his chin in his hands and raised his eyebrows at Miss Palmer. There was silence for a while and then he spoke.

"Michael," he said. "Mr. Archer has gone. What is said in this room will stay in this room. Do you understand?"

I nodded.

"What happened, Michael?"

"I tripped over some tree roots, sir. Got the cake all over me, banged my nose. Jamie had nothing to do with it. Honest."

Mr. Atkins nodded slowly. He didn't look at all surprised. Just sad.

· · ·

They sent me home. I didn't want to go, but Miss Palmer gave me no choice. She said it was her duty of care when a head injury was involved. I couldn't remember my phone number. It had only been connected a couple of days. So Miss Palmer rang Dad on his mobile—he'd given them that when he'd enrolled me—and he gave permission to send me home in a taxi. I'd hoped to keep all this between Mary and me. It was a dim hope, and now it had been totally blown.

"Fell over a tree, eh, Michael?" Mary said after I had repeated the story I'd given Miss Palmer.

"Yeah," I said.

"Face-first into a piece of chocolate cake?"

"Yup."

"Must have been funny."

"I guess so."

"Shocking waste of cake, though."

We both laughed then. That's the thing with Mary. She doesn't push me. She knew all right. But she also understood I wouldn't talk about it, and she respected that. Sometimes I don't know what I'd do without her.

Dad, however, was not happy when he came home from work.

"You're there five bloody minutes! Jesus Christ, Michael. What happened? And don't give me that crap about tree roots again, 'cause I don't buy it. Someone picked on you because you're fat, right? Did you fight back? Nah. Come on. Tell me."

I shrugged, kept my head down, and pushed lettuce around my plate. If I said nothing, he'd get angrier. If I told the truth, he'd be even worse. He'd go on for hours about how I was a coward and he was ashamed of me. Mary tried to help out.

"Leave him alone, Joe. He doesn't want to talk about it. It was his first day, for God's sake, and he's upset."

Dad flung down his knife and fork.

"Will you bloody answer me?"

"I told you. I fell," I said.

"Drop it, Joe. Please?" said Mary.

Dad picked up his knife and fork again.

"I don't know what's the matter with you. I've tried to get you to do judo or karate lessons. I've taught you a bit of boxing. If you fight, you avoid trouble; that's all I'm saying. With some of these bastards, a good hiding would solve a lot of their problems. They'd think twice about bullying then."

"I don't want to fight, Dad."

Dad pointed his fork at me.

"Then lose some weight. Sitting there like a whale. It's disgusting. No wonder you get bullied. You can't expect kids not to give you shit. I'm not saying it's right, because it isn't. I'm just saying you've got to expect it. And there are two answers to the problem. You gotta fight back or lose weight. It's that simple."

"It's not that simple, Joe," said Mary. "It's not."

Dad flung his knife and fork down again.

"I'm sick of this. Everywhere we go, it's the same. I'm bloody ashamed of you."

"You don't mean that, Joe. And if you're sick of it, how do you think he feels?"

Dad pushed his plate away and got to his feet.

"I don't give a crap. That's it. Get bullied but don't whine to me."

I had never whined to him. I never would. But there was no point saying anything. So I sat, eyes on the lettuce, while he put his jacket on.

"I'm going to the pub," he said. "And you can clean this dinner crap up. It's all you're good for, God knows."

After the door slammed, we sat there for a while. Mary reached over and ran her hand through my hair.

"He doesn't mean it, Michael. He's had a bad first day at work. Makes two of you, doesn't it? Hey, come on. Cheer up. Tell me more about that nice girl you met at school today. That's good, isn't it?"

Yeah, I thought. A possible friend. And two definite enemies. When I added it up, the math wasn't good.

4.

"How did you get my number?" I asked.

"From Mr. Atkins. I said it was an emergency. I promised I wouldn't let anyone know what he'd done." Leah giggled. "He's a good guy."

"He seems like it," I said.

"Anyway, sorry to be ringing so late. Hey, I'm glad it was you who picked up. I'm not sure what I would have done if it had been your mum or dad."

Dad wasn't back from the pub, and Mary must have gone to bed. She wasn't around anyway. I was sitting in my favorite place—the laundry steps—listening to Leah on the cordless. I was amazed she'd gone to the trouble of ringing. It was the first phone call I'd had in . . . Well, I couldn't remember how long. I tried to keep the excitement out of my voice.

"Anyway," she continued, "I heard what happened today. That Martin is such a bastard. Are you okay, Michael?"

I twisted the telephone cord between my fingers.

"Sure," I said. "No big deal."

"I don't want you thinking we're all like him. There are plenty of kids who think what he did to you was shitty. I guess I wanted you to know that before you went to sleep. That you're not alone."

Normally, I'm so focused on looking for differences, they don't take me by surprise. But occasionally, when they do sneak up on me, they're the big ones. I knew something was wrong. When I realized what it was, I nearly laughed. I twisted the cord some more.

"Leah," I said. "Do you want a real experience, something that will blow your mind?"

There was a pause, and I knew she was sifting my words for the sinister or the unpleasant. "What do you mean, Michael?" she said eventually.

"Have you ever flown?"

"Well, I've flown to Sydney a couple of times."

"No," I said. "No, I don't mean that. I mean flying. Like a bird."

There was an embarrassed laugh at the other end. "Yeah,

well, it's getting late, so I'd better let you get to bed. I'll see you at school tomorrow. . . ."

"Put the phone down, Leah. I don't mean hang up. Place the receiver on the floor next to you. And don't be frightened. Whatever happens."

"Michael . . ."

"Humor me, Leah. Please?"

I heard a sigh. Under normal circumstances, she would have hung up. But I knew she'd do as I asked. She didn't have a choice. This was my world. I had control.

I heard the dull thud as she placed the phone on the floor. I didn't need to check, but it's a habit. Sure enough, there were three laundry steps instead of two. The cordless phone was cordless again. I centered myself, found the calm at my core, and willed it all to happen.

My body dissolved around the edges, slowly at first, but gathering momentum. I watched myself from the outside. Within moments, I had become smoke, a faintly glowing cloud above the steps. And then I poured myself through the holes in the mouthpiece, a genie disappearing into a bottle, until all that was left was the phone rocking gently on the ground.

I had never been inside a phone before. It was strange.

My understanding of electronics is hazy at the best of times, and I have no idea how a cordless phone works. But it's all improvisation, I suppose.

I found myself racing through a wire. It twisted and snaked as I sped down it at breathtaking speed. The colors—reds, yellows, and greens—became tracks, continuous lines that appeared stationary only because of my relative speed. I was in a white plastic tunnel, the strips of color an aurora over me.

A bend loomed and then I was past it, hurtling down another straight. I was under the earth. There was soil around me and growing things, thick roots seeking water and life. Then I was traveling up, across streets, ignoring hundreds of intersections I knew weren't right. No map needed. Pinpricks of light rushed toward me. I streamed through the receiver. The smoke that was my body drifted and solidified. I smiled at Leah.

"Just thought I'd drop in," I said.

She didn't seem surprised. I must have wanted it that way, though I wasn't aware of making it so. She tilted her head.

"You mentioned something about flying?" she said.

"Sure," I said, taking her by the hand. "Seat belts on and turn off all electronic appliances. We have clearance."

I liked the way her hair curled under her chin. I liked the pajamas she was wearing—silly kids' sleepwear with bright embroidered teddy bears. She smelled freshly showered and her skin glowed. And her eyes. I felt I could fall into those eyes and never hit bottom.

"Will you give me an explanation, Captain?" she said.

"Compliments of the airline," I said as we lifted off the ground.

• • •

It was a good flight. I didn't try any fancy stuff, like diving toward the ground and stopping millimeters from impact, or flying into an electrical storm, riding the lightning. We just drifted, circling above the city. A full moon, impossibly large, bathed us in light. Stars sprinkled the sky, millions upon millions of points. We rode the breeze like birds, cushioned the air, floated as if in a pool. Our arms stretched out around us, we watched the blaze of other worlds. Leah's hand was in mine. She wasn't holding on too tight. In fact, sometimes she let her hand slip a little, so we were connected only by the slightest brushing of fingertips. All was calm.

We flew over the coast and swooped over the boats moored in the bay. It might have been minutes, or hours. Eventually, we spiraled down toward the school. It seemed as good a place as any to sit and talk. The security lights dotted around the outside walkway softened the harsh angles of the buildings.

We landed on top of the science block, an expanse of dark asphalt bordered by a low wall no more than a meter in height. Leah and I sat on the edge, our feet dangling over the drop. For a few minutes we studied the city in silence. Lights sparkled in the distance, and we could see the darkness where sea met land. It was quiet. A slight breeze brought the taste of salt and gasoline. Leah sighed.

"Incredible," she said.

"It is," I replied. "And you know the best part? This is just the beginning. All your dreams laid out before you. No limits, unless there are limits on the imagination. It's a miracle."

Leah reached out and took my hand.

"You promised an explanation," she said.

If I'd thought about it too much, I would have laughed. Locked in my own head, explaining to myself. Then again, I'd spent most of my life doing just that.

"Have you heard of lucid dreaming?" I said.

Leah frowned. "I know what *lucid* means," she said. "It means 'clear' or 'well-spoken.' I've no idea what it has to do with dreaming."

"Clear dreaming. Controlled dreaming. That's what it's about. Knowing you are in a dream and being able to shape it."

"I don't understand."

I swung my right leg over and straddled the wall, facing her.

"Most people dream but don't remember much afterward. Maybe the vivid ones, and the nightmares, stay with you for a while. But it's like a tendril of smoke. You wake and the dreams fade. In moments, the details are gone, diluted by the rush of the real world. A drop of brilliant color in a colorless sea. Swallowed. Gone."

Leah nodded.

"I'm not like that," I continued. "I remember my dreams. Every detail. But more than that, I know when I'm in a dream. Have you ever known, while you were dreaming, that you were asleep?"

She thought carefully. "I don't think so. I can't remember."

"Well, that's where the power lies. When you know you're actually dreaming, the shock often wakes you. But if you keep that knowledge and still hold the dream, then you can control it. You can do whatever you want. No limits."

Leah shook her head slowly. I grabbed her by the shoulders and fixed my eyes on hers.

"I'll show you," I said as I toppled us both from the ledge and into nothingness.

The world swept up to meet us. I felt the rush of air whipping my clothes against my body, my stomach churning. And then I leveled out, turned up to the sky. This time I traveled fast. I had one arm around Leah's waist, holding her close to me, the other stretched straight up. Pathetic, I know, but sometimes it's good to do things with style. The ground was shrinking at an incredible rate. I could just make out the sea framing the shape of Australia and then the curvature of Earth itself. We exploded into blackness. The bright dust of stars was all around. Then the bone-white disk leapt up to meet us. I slowed and settled, my feet sending a trail of dust arcing gently in the vacuum. I set Leah onto her feet, took her by the hand, and tugged her down next to me. We sat and turned toward the sphere, green and blue and white, hanging against its black backdrop.

I never tired of its beauty. One half was golden in sunlight, and we could make out the shape of Africa and a wedge of South America shrouded in cloud. A line divided Earth, one half hidden in night. We sat, bathed in earthlight.

"I look for differences," I said. "In a dream, there will always be something strange, something illogical. A cordless phone that has a cord, a blade of grass that behaves in a way that is impossible. When I recognize the difference, I know I am in the world of my imagination. The rest is simply what I will to happen."

Leah kept her face toward the Earth. She said nothing for a minute or two.

"So this isn't me sitting here," she said finally. "It's your dream of me."

"Right," I said. "That's right. The real you is asleep somewhere down there. Or maybe not. You might be watching TV or reading a book. I don't know. All I know is that I'm asleep, lying in my bed, and that has let me into this world, a world where I can travel down a telephone wire. A world where we can fly to the moon."

"So I can't possibly remember this." It wasn't a question.

"There's nothing for you to remember. But *I'll* remember it, this time we've shared. I'll remember flying with Leah. It'll help me through the day, the real world, where none of this is possible."

Leah giggled.

"So you're like Superman! Quiet, unassuming Michael Terny during the day, but a lord of creation at night."

"I'm a Dreamrider," I said. "If I want to, I can plan everything, down to the last detail. Most times, I don't. I control, but

I also let my world do what it wants. I set some events in motion and then see where they take me. I ride the Dream."

"It's not real."

"It's better than real. Real is overrated."

We sat a while longer, not needing to say much. But I knew it was all on the point of ending, that if I turned, I would see it. The glass. I could feel it pressing on me, a solid force a few meters behind my shoulder blades.

And then depression came like a weight. It always happened like this, the joy of freedom soured by the price to be paid. The glass.

I couldn't control it. I controlled everything else. *Everything* else. But at the end, always at the end, it was there. Nothing could keep me from it. My gateway back to the real world. I watched Leah and tried to keep her there by force of will. But she was fading. Already I could see the paleness of the moon through her. When she turned toward me, there were stars in her hair. It was pointless, but I tried to firm her, flesh out her figure, keep her whole.

But the stars only brightened. Darkness was eating her. Within a minute she had gone, dissolved into nothingness. I hadn't even said goodbye. There was no point. I looked back out at the Earth. It was as if I was alone in the universe. The stars were cold and distant. In the whole of existence there was nothing but me and darkness.

Finally, I turned. Now that control was gone, there was no point delaying. Time to wake up. But I had to go through this first. I could sit and watch and refuse to turn. I could do that until it seemed enough hours had passed for the stars themselves to crumble. Time has no meaning in the Dream. It is a different clock that ticks here. But I had to go back. So I turned.

The glass was featureless, as always, apart from the pale tinge of my reflection. I moved my hand toward it and felt the thudding in my chest deepen until it was a roaring in my ears. A trickle of sweat ran down my right cheek. A burst of orange came from the left corner. Something shifted in the glass. Movement. A familiar shape. I felt on the verge of recognition.

And then there was only darkness and the sound of my lungs tearing and gulping at the air.

Tuesday

1.

The alarm clock said 6:55 a.m. I waited until the beating of my heart faded to a thin pulse, then got up and rummaged through the wardrobe. The tactic yesterday hadn't worked, but I picked out another anonymous T-shirt and plain shorts. I showered, dressed, and went through to the kitchen.

I made a pot of tea and poured myself a cup. Dad, I remembered, had said something about an early shift, but I hadn't heard him leave. Mary was nowhere to be seen either, though the kitchen door was open. I knew she was wandering the garden, having her first smoke of the day. She didn't smoke when Dad was home. He hated the smell. So the first thing she did when he left the house was light up. She reeked of smoke, but he chose not to comment. Maybe he thought that if he kept quiet, she wouldn't smoke as much. I didn't know. It wasn't something we were ever likely to discuss.

I found an open packet of bacon in the fridge and put a rasher under the grill. Dad would definitely notice if I took more, and that would mean another argument about my weight. He'd probably notice anyway. Mary would be cool. She cared about my diet, but she wasn't too fussy. That was the way things worked for Mary and me—I kept her smoking habit to myself, and she did the same for my occasional rasher of bacon. It was one of the things that made us so close—the secrets we kept from a common enemy.

"How do you feel about today, Michael?"

Her voice startled me. I was watching the rasher sink into the butter on my bread. Mary leaned against the door, a cigarette in one hand and a cup of tea in the other. She gave me a kind smile as I brought the sandwich to my mouth.

"You can always have the day off," she continued. "It would be understandable, and your dad wouldn't have to know." We both knew, however, that he would find out. He always did.

"Thanks, Mary," I said, taking that first delicious bite. "But it won't be any easier if I don't go in."

"Like riding a bike and all that?"

"Exactly," I said.

• • •

The bus stop was a five-minute walk from the house, but I gave myself plenty of time. I was hoping Leah would get on, but I had no idea if she lived on my route or even if she took the bus at all. It was a beautiful day, and the short walk made me feel better. I was nervous, obviously. That never really went away, even after I'd been at a school for months. But something about the quality of the air, the way the sun shone through the leaves on the trees, made me glad to be there, walking at that particular place, at that particular time. It's difficult to explain.

It was quiet at the bus stop. I had gone early to miss the rush, and only a couple of kids were waiting. Judging by their uniforms, they didn't go to my school anyway. When the bus arrived, I had nearly all the seating to choose from. The back row was out. Kids who sit at the back of buses don't ask you to move politely. I sat behind the driver. There were no safe spots, but I stood the most chance of avoiding hassle there.

Martin got on at the first stop. He swung up onto the bus with a bunch of other boys and flashed his card at the driver. For a moment I thought he would pass by. I kept my head turned, as if watching something out the window. But then I felt a thump on the vinyl next to me.

"Hey, Michael," he said. "It is Michael, isn't it?"

I remembered what he'd said about answering questions.

"Yes. Michael Terny."

He grinned. "Well, Michael Terny, I'm Martin Leechy. It's good to see you again. Put it there."

He held out his hand. I didn't feel comfortable taking it, but I didn't have much choice. Once again, he shook my hand firmly.

"Look, Michael," he said. "I want to apologize about yesterday. I feel bad. You had every right to rat me out. But you didn't and I want to say thanks."

I shrugged.

"Well, it's good of you to take that attitude. I appreciate it. I really do," he said.

I turned back to the window, hoping he would leave. Martin whistled tunelessly for a while, drumming his fingers on the edge of the seat. Then he tapped me on the arm.

"The thing is, Michael, I've got a question, and I was wondering if you'd mind answering it."

I stared at the back of the driver's head.

"You see, you really are enormously fat, Michael, and I was wondering how you got that way. Do you just shovel in food from morning to night? Is that it? Or do you take something? Tablets of some kind?"

I looked down at my knees.

Martin continued. His tone was friendly and relaxed, like he was discussing a football game with a mate. "Maybe you do the reverse of that procedure? What do they call it? When they stick a tube in your guts and it sucks out the fat? Do you go along from time to time and get everybody else's fat pumped into you? What is it, Mikey? Are we talking nature or nurture here?"

"Liposuction," I said.

Martin slapped his forehead with his hand.

"That's it! Damn. Memory like a sieve!"

I knew then that Martin was going to be more dangerous than other bullies I'd come up against. It had to do with intelligence. Most of the kids who made my life hell were no-hopers, their insults routine and unimaginative. But Martin was smart. The "nature/nurture" remark told me that. Of course, smart kids had bullied me too, but normally they were trying to impress their mates. And sometimes there would be shame in their eyes as they did it. But Martin had no audience. I didn't know how to deal with his friendly hatred.

The bus pulled to a stop and Leah got on. She flashed her card and was almost past me when she noticed us.

"Hey, Michael," she said. "How are you?"

Martin gave a broad smile.

"Wassup, Leah. How ya doin'?"

She gave a tight smile and a slight nod.

"Listen, guys," said Martin, "I'd love to stay and chat, but there's a group at the back who need my input. You know how it is—you can't spread yourself too thinly. Isn't that right, Michael? So I'll love you and leave you. Here you go, Leah. Have my seat. Not that there's a great deal of it. You have to hang your buttock over the edge, but I suppose you two know all about hanging buttocks, right? Take care. Later, eh, Michael?"

Leah sat down and I felt the tension drain away. I'm grateful for small victories. Another confrontation avoided, or at least postponed.

"I dreamed about you last night," she said.

"Yeah?"

"Yeah." She blushed slightly. "Not like . . . you know, that sort of dream. I don't mean . . ."

"I'm interested in dreams," I said. "What was it about?"

She shrugged. "I have real problems remembering dreams. It's hazy. I was somewhere high with you and we talked. That's it. At least, that's all I remember, but it was a vivid dream. It had to be. They're the only kind that linger the following day."

That was interesting. A coincidence, for sure, but I'd give it some thought.

"Anyway," she continued, "I heard about what happened yesterday. Are you all right? That Martin . . . God, he is such a bastard. Thinks he's so tough and funny. What was he doing sitting next to you? Giving you a hard time?"

I shrugged.

"Not really," I said. "It's all right. Don't worry about it."

She looked at me closely. I liked the way her hair flipped under her chin. I liked her plumpness. But it was her eyes more than anything. I'm a sucker for eyes.

"Listen, Michael," she said. "He gives you crap, you let someone know. Don't let him get away with it. Promise me you'll tell someone."

"We're here," I said. The bus had stopped outside the school gates, and kids were crowding the aisles, jostling each other. I picked up my bag.

"Come on," I said. "Let's see if I can get through an entire day."

"Michael, let's see if you can get through an entire day," said Mr. Atkins.

He'd called me over at the beginning of Home Group. I had a bad feeling he was going to cross-examine me about yesterday, but his eyes were relaxed and smiling.

"I'm proud of you, my boy," he continued. "Falling into a chocolate cake within half a day of starting. That has to be some kind of record. And I want you to know that, having done so, you are maintaining the very high standards of Home Group Fifteen. In fact, you have enhanced our already considerable reputation for active stupidity, and for that you deserve congratulations."

He took off his glasses and chewed the end of one arm. It was already pitted with teeth marks.

"You don't have anything to tell me, do you, Michael?" he added. "Now you've had a chance to sleep on it?"

"No, sir. I don't think so."

He sighed. "No. I didn't think so either."

There was a flash of tiredness in his eyes. I'd noticed it yesterday. I knew he was struggling to keep something hidden, his sense of humor a guard against it. He put his glasses on the desk.

"Michael, I am excessively old, and I have been teaching for more years than is good for me. I have a theory that the more time you spend with young people, the less you understand them. The less you are capable of understanding. I have no idea what interests young people anymore. I know nothing about the music you listen to, the films you watch, the technology you use. To be honest, I have no idea how my alarm clock works, let alone mobile phones and instant messaging. But for all that, I am a good listener. Maybe because I don't know anything at all about you, I'm a better listener. Do you understand what I mean?"

I nodded but he didn't seem satisfied.

"Put very simply," he added, "if you ever want to talk about anything to someone who is not going to make judgments, then you might do worse than talk to me. I'm too old to be judgmental."

"Thanks, sir," I said. "You're a very kind man."

Mr. Atkins's eyes widened. He frowned for a moment, as if trying to decide whether I was sending him up. Then he laughed.

"Well, Michael," he said. "Maybe I'm not the only one around here who is too old-fashioned for his own good. 'Kind,' eh? Do you know . . . I think you are correct. I am kind. Use my kindness, if you feel so inclined. All right?"

I nodded.

Mr. Atkins, almost absentmindedly, reached out a hand, and a coin blinked into existence. He rolled it over the back of his hand, flipping it along the ridges of his knuckles. Then the coin vanished. He turned his hand over, palm up, and there was nothing there. Then he clenched his fist and the coin reappeared, cartwheeling back and forth. I kept my eyes glued to his hand, but I couldn't see how he did it. Mr. Atkins continued to speak, as if his magic show was of no importance.

"Tell me, Michael. Are you coming to the Year Ten Social this Friday?"

"The Social?"

"An esteemed tradition in the hallowed halls of Millways High School. A time when all the Year Tens get together for a night of unbridled disco dancing in the school hall. A time for liaisons with members of the opposite sex. A time for, dare one say it, smuggled grog, the occasional fight, and releasing the grip on the old testosterone. A social."

"I don't think so, sir."

"And why not?" The coin vanished, then appeared in his left hand. I couldn't tear my eyes away.

"I'm not really built for disco dancing, sir."

"Who is? It's always struck me as a singularly unnatural

activity and is one I have avoided assiduously and successfully. But that doesn't mean you can't come along just for the . . . well, the social element, I suppose. Come on, Michael. The people who know about such things assure me a splendid time is had by all. And I have it on reliable authority that this year is going to be remarkable. A 'themed horror' event. Give it a go, eh?"

"I'll think about it, sir."

"Do that. Give it serious thought." He picked up his glasses and put them on. "And now I'm afraid a pile of Year Nine argumentative essays awaits me."

Mr. Atkins flexed his fingers as if preparing them for the task at hand. There was no sign of the coin. I instinctively patted my pockets, but they were empty.

"No doubt," he continued, "I'll be shocked by the poverty of intellect and the complete disregard for the most rudimentary elements of English grammar, but, as the saying goes, they won't mark themselves. Have a good day, Michael." He fixed me with his gaze. "That's a direct instruction."

"Thanks, sir." I nodded. "Sir?"

Mr. Atkins peered over the top of his glasses.

"How do you do that, sir? The thing with the coin."

He leaned back in the chair and locked his hands behind his head.

"Ah, Michael. The secret is to practice. Practice and persevere. If you stick at something, you get better. At the start, you make mistakes. You stumble and fail. But keep on at it and suddenly the trick becomes second nature to you. You don't know how you couldn't do it before. If you practice, you can make the impossible seem easy. Think about it, my boy."

I smiled. I knew he wasn't talking only about the coin. My own experiences in the Dream were proof of what he had said. Maybe I could apply the same determination to the real world. I'd think about it.

There were only ten minutes left of Home Group. Kids were sitting around chatting. A few were playing handheld computer games, but most were in small groups. Leah was with the same knot of girls I'd seen yesterday. I watched from the corner of my eyes. I like to people-watch, carefully. Some people find it annoying. After a few moments, Leah came over.

"Hey," she said.

"Listen," I said, keeping my voice low. "You don't have to look after me all the time, you know. I'm not a charity case. I'll be fine."

"Get over yourself, will you?" She flicked hair out from under her chin. Irritation flashed in her eyes. "If I didn't want to talk to you, I wouldn't. Okay?"

I kept my head down. "Okay," I said. "Sorry."

"So what was old Atkins going on about?"

"The Social."

"Are you going?"

"Doubt it."

"Why?"

"Not my kind of thing."

"Oh, come on. It'll be fun. Honest. It's like one of the biggest things at Millways, the Year Ten Social. Everyone goes. And it's not one of those daggy things with a crap DJ and about five people dancing while the others just stand around. I'm serious. It's planned by the Student Council and everything. Great music, great food. And it's themed this year."

"So I heard."

"Yeah. Fright Night. Doesn't have to be anything complicated. You know, just a bit of fake blood, dagger in the head sort of thing. Look, it sounds crap, the way I'm explaining it, but it isn't. It's fun. You should come."

Leah was all animated. I didn't want to give the impression I was boring.

"I'll think about it," I said.

"Don't think; just say yes. And if you're worried that I'll be at your side the entire time, pestering you, then I promise I won't. If you want, I'll ignore you the whole night. Okay?"

She smiled at me and I smiled back. I loved her smile. It came from deep inside.

"Leah?" I said. "What is it with Mr. Atkins?"

"Mr. Atkins? What do you mean? He's a good guy. A really cool teacher."

"Yeah, but he's worried about something. I can see it in his eyes."

Leah glanced toward the teacher's desk. Mr. Atkins was hunched over a bunch of papers, red pen scribbling furiously, a tic twitching over his right eye. Whatever he was reading, it wasn't giving him pleasure. I had to smile. Leah sighed. Then she leaned in closer.

"Listen," she whispered. "You are not to repeat this, right? Do you promise, Michael?"

I nodded.

"Well, I heard two teachers talking on yard duty. About Mr. Atkins's wife. I *think* it was about her. I didn't get all of it, but they said something about cancer and not having much time left. I can't swear to it, Michael. But it would fit. Mr. Atkins has changed recently. Oh, he still has the same personality, but it's like he has to force it now. As if he's worried."

The bell rang and I didn't get a chance to reply. I had science first up and Leah had art. I paused for a moment in the doorway and looked back at Mr. Atkins.

He was chewing the ends of his glasses again and staring out the window. Something in his expression suggested that whatever he was seeing was far beyond the school buildings, the oval, or the clear blue sky.

2.

At lunchtime I headed for the oval, but Jamie Archer got to me first. He was with a group of mates, and I tried to slip past, but he grabbed me by the shirt and pushed me up against the gym wall.

"What's the rush, Wrenbury?" he said. "You and me have got some shit to settle. When d'ya reckon'd be a good time? Now? After school?"

I avoided his eyes, but his mates were circling me, eager, expectant. My mouth went dry and sweat trickled down my belly.

"I don't want trouble," I said. I tried to say it with confidence, but my voice was hoarse. It came out trembling with fear. Jamie pushed his face closer to mine. My vision filled with the redness of his hair.

"Don't you?" he said, his voice soft. "Well, that's strange. See, I know what happened on the oval yesterday. I saw it. And I don't care whether you want trouble or not, 'cause I reckon you got it."

"Is there a problem here, Mr. Archer?"

Suddenly the circle broke and Mr. Atkins was in front of me. Jamie let go of my shirt and carefully brushed me down, as if getting rid of wrinkles.

"No, sir," said Jamie. "Just getting acquainted with the new boy. Isn't that right, new boy?"

I nodded. Mr. Atkins gave a small shake of his head.

"Excellent," he said. He sounded bright and cheerful, but his eyes told a different story. "That is very public-spirited of you, Mr. Archer. You embody all that has made Millways what it is today, and I won't forget it. Trust me on that. However, there is only so much bonhomie I can tolerate on my yard duty, so I suggest you and your friends move on now. Spread the good cheer, Jamie."

Jamie smiled but it was thin.

"Sure, sir. No problem, sir. Guess I'll catch you later, eh, new boy?"

"His name is Michael, Mr. Archer," said Mr. Atkins. We watched as Jamie strolled off. He sat on a wall about ten meters away, his friends ranged on either side. They stared back at us.

"Do something, Michael," said Mr. Atkins. His voice didn't carry far. "Do something."

"I've got to go," I said. "Thanks, sir."

I made my way to the tree I had found yesterday. Throughout the walk, eyes were an itch in the small of my back. I sat against the gnarled trunk and unpacked my lunch. Two Tim Tams, but the rest was boring—a salad sandwich, an apple, and low-fat rice crackers. I ate slowly, gazing out over the oval. Time passed. Four or five wedge-tailed kites hovered, riding the air lazily. The sky was sharp, the trees were hard-edged, the clouds cutout shapes. The scene was a child's drawing, all primary colors.

One of the kites swooped toward me, and it was a bird in two dimensions. Turning, it was as thin as paper, a black line against impossible blue. I looked at my sandwich. It bulged with meat. I pried open the two halves of bread. The thick slabs of meat were drenched in gravy. I replaced the bread and bit into it. The taste flooded my body with pleasure.

I brushed crumbs off my lap and stood. What was I going to do with this time? I felt, briefly, the urge to find Jamie, but the moment passed. I'd had enough of violence. Time for something different.

The school's administration section was busy, but I passed through it unseen. A filing cabinet in an inner office gave me the address of Atkins, Keith. I memorized it and left. It didn't take long to find the house either. It was only a ten-minute walk from school. I stood outside the front gates.

It was a big house showing signs of age. Paint was peeling from the weatherboards, and the garden was sprinkled with weeds. A large dog basked in a pool of sunshine by the front door. There was no sign of anyone. I opened the gate and the dog jumped up, a low growl building in its throat. In real life I would have been frightened. The dog's hackles rose and its lips curled back, revealing yellow teeth. I've always been scared of big dogs, even if they can't harm me. This one stared right through me, like I was something dimly sensed. It was unnerving. I felt like a ghost. I suppose in a way I was.

I skirted the dog and knocked on the door. For a while it appeared that no one was home. I knocked again and the sound resounded through the house. I didn't want to just open the door and go in. Manners are important, even in the Dream. Finally, I heard a faint sound from inside. Someone was coming. There was a shuffling sound, as if someone old was moving, slowly and painfully. I thought about leaving then. It's impossible to intrude on your own dreams, yet that's how I felt. An intruder. But I didn't leave.

The door opened. A thin, frail woman stood like an old person, as if bent by an invisible weight. Her hair was thin, wispy, and faded, like something left too long in the sun, but when I looked at her face, I knew she couldn't have been more than fifty. Her skin was baggy, yet it was her eyes that held my attention. She had deep and kind eyes, but the pain under the surface made me flinch. It was like seeing calm water and catching a glimpse of monsters beneath. It was such an arresting face that I stood for some time before I noticed she was watching me with amused patience. I cleared my throat.

"Mrs. Atkins?" I said.

"Yes. What can I do for you?"

"My name is Michael Terny, Mrs. Atkins. I am one of your husband's students."

She gave a small smile.

"Well, Michael, I'm pleased to meet you, but I think you'll find my husband is at school. Can I ask why you are not there too?"

I felt uncomfortable under her gaze. This Dream seemed different from normal. In the early days of lucid dreaming, I hadn't had much control. The Dream had its own logic, and I could only influence minor details. It had been a long time since that had happened. I could shape everything now. True, I would often allow the Dream to flow in the surreal manner of ordinary dreams. But even that was a conscious choice to let go. Not now, though. The dog and Mrs. Atkins appeared to be independent of me in some way. It was strange, but I had come this far and I wanted to know what would happen.

"Mrs. Atkins, I am not here to see your husband. I have come to see you. To help you."

She gave a tired smile, as if a child had said something cute. But it was impossible to take offense.

"Well, Michael, that is very kind of you. I'm not at all sure I need your help, but do come in and tell me more." She stood aside and I moved past her into the hall.

"First door on the right," she said. "Make yourself comfortable and I'll put the kettle on."

I went into the living room. There was a couch against the window and a couple of easy chairs, both threadbare. The room was lined with bookcases. Every bit of wall space was taken up with rows and rows of books. It was like a library. I squeezed past the coffee table in front of the couch and sat down. The air was dusty, the smell of musty paper thick in the room. It was wonderful, calm, reassuring.

I looked at the books on the shelves. Mrs. Atkins came in with a teapot and two cups on a tray. She moved carefully, as if afraid of breaking herself, then put the tray down and sat with a small sigh. I poured the tea and she didn't protest. She took a cup, sat back, and closed her eyes. There was a bowl of old-fashioned sugar cubes. I liked their hardness beneath my fingers. I put four lumps into my tea. On impulse, I dropped one into the top pocket of my shirt. Mrs. Atkins sipped her tea, leaned forward, and put the cup back on the coffee table.

"You're sick," I said.

She gave a small laugh. "Well, Michael," she said, "you're not wrong there. I think I can safely say that."

"I can help you."

"I don't need your help, Michael. My husband gives me all the help I need."

"I don't mean that," I said. "I mean I can help with your illness."

She looked at me and there was a twinkle in her eyes.

"My illness?" she said. "Well, Michael, that is indeed kind of you. But I'm afraid there is not much you can do. There's nothing anyone can do. I've consulted more doctors than you have probably seen in your entire life. So I appreciate your offer, but . . ."

"You have a brain tumor," I said.

The twinkle disappeared. She turned to face me, and I saw the beginnings of anger in her eyes.

"Has my husband been talking to you? If he has been talking about me to his students . . ."

"I can see it, Mrs. Atkins," I said. I could too. There was a dark mass under her skull, above her right eye. "If you'll just sit back and close your eyes, I'll get rid of it."

For a moment I thought her anger was going to flare. Emotions struggled across her face. Then, abruptly, she smiled and her face cleared. Maybe I wanted her to see me as a harmless lunatic. Maybe I'd decided she had nothing left to lose, not even dignity.

"Faith healing, is it, Michael?"

"Something like that," I said.

She leaned back and closed her eyes, the smile still there. I put my hands on her skull. It felt frail, as if with only a little pressure I could break through bone and tissue and put my hands on the brain beneath. And that's what I did. I pressed gently and my hands parted flesh and bone like water. I could feel the tumor beneath my fingers. It felt hard and there was something about it that made my skin crawl.

I moved my hands around the growth and felt its attachment to the tissue beneath. I could also sense rather than feel the other knots of cancer spreading from it, an infection staining her brain.

I can't explain how I did it. In the Dream things work differently. I didn't tear the cancer away. I willed it to be gone. I put my mind into my hands. Gradually, the tumor separated from the healthy tissue and gathered in my palms. When I was sure I had it all, I removed my hands. The skull flowed beneath my fingers and closed behind them. The whole thing took less than a minute. Mrs. Atkins lay with her eyes closed, a dreamy look on her face.

"It's done, Mrs. Atkins," I said. "It's gone."

She opened her eyes and her expression was dazed. She put her hands slowly to her head. I knew something felt different to her. An expression of wonder passed across her face, like a burden had been lifted. Or maybe something added. Wholeness, perhaps, or a sense of cleanliness where before there had been contamination. She shook her head slightly and her fingers clenched. She stared at me.

"It *has* gone, Mrs. Atkins," I said. "Believe me."

Not that her belief had anything to do with it.

"Well, I've taken up enough of your time," I said. "I'd best get back to school."

She rose carefully, but I could tell she was surprised by how easy it was. We walked to the door.

"You're a strange boy, Michael," she said. Then she put out her hand and I shook it. "But I want to thank you. Truly."

"Take care, Mrs. Atkins," I said.

I walked off. I needed to get back to my body, lying under a tree on the school oval. I could have done that instantly, but I didn't feel like it. I walked back slowly, feeling the sunshine on my legs and arms. My body was singing.

When I reached the edge of the school oval, I could see, in the distance, my huddled shape under the tree. I had done this many times, but there was always a jolt, a sense of overwhelming strangeness, when I closed on my sleeping body. I walked on until I was standing over myself. Mounds of flesh hung under my chin. My T-shirt was slightly rucked, exposing rolls of pale belly. I saw myself the way others saw me, and I shared their disgust. I *was* disgusting. That's why the Dream is so good. I can be what I want to be. Back in that huge, unwieldy body I am trapped. But in the end, there's never a choice. I always have to return.

I turned to face what couldn't be avoided. The glass filled my vision, an expanse of darkness. The urge to reach out and touch its surface was irresistible. In my mind, I could see the ripples I would create, my hand stirring its curve, sinking, finger by finger, into black depths. I could see my hand stretch slowly toward it.

But I knew what would happen, what always happened. Maybe I got closer this time. It seemed that each Dream brought my fingers closer to the surface, that it was only a matter of time before I would touch it. More—that it was important, even vital, to make contact. The flash of yellow came from the top right-hand corner. My hand flinched as if from a flame. Beads of perspiration broke out on my forehead. My heart raced. The yellow flashed across the glass toward the bottom left-hand corner, then dimmed. In that brief instant, I could see a shape moving within the surface. I felt its panic. Then, with a dull roar, like a far-off explosion, the colors pumped toward me—deep orange, mingled with fire red and harsh, violent yellows. They came in waves, as if to swallow me. I tried to scream, but no sound came. For a moment there was nothing but blazing colors. They swamped the world.

My body jerked into a sitting position and my eyes snapped open. I felt the stiffness of my limbs. A string of drool was draped over my chin. My body was a frightening weight. I had difficulty raising myself up on an elbow. It always happened like this. It was as if I was in someone else's body, dragging a strange carcass.

After a few moments, my heart slowed and breathing

became easier. I noticed that someone had pinned a note to the leg of my shorts. It read "Beeched whale." Not Martin, I thought. He wouldn't make a spelling mistake like that.

Jamie.

The oval stretched out around me. I forced my eyes, heavy with sleep, to look at my watch. I had slept through twenty minutes of the afternoon's first lesson. No one had woken me. Why should they? It must have given them a good laugh. I didn't feel like laughing. Not when I saw that the oval wasn't quite deserted. One person was watching as I struggled to my feet, plucking the note from my shorts. Miss Palmer, the assistant principal, was walking toward me.

I hadn't made the best start at Millways High.

3.

"I don't care that you fell asleep, Michael." Miss Palmer ran her hands through her hair. Her eyes were tired. "Though, having said that, you need to make sure you're getting a decent night's sleep. Are you drinking enough water?"

I nodded.

"It's the note that bothers me. This is exactly the kind of bullying I was talking about. Let me ask you again—do you know who wrote it?"

I shrugged.

"I'll find out. Even if I have to check the handwriting of every student. I won't let this behavior go unpunished in my school."

I wanted to tell her to forget it, that a fuss was only going to make my life more difficult. But I didn't. She kept me in her office until the start of the last lesson. That was okay. I didn't like the idea of going into class halfway through. So I turned up to Social Studies, hoping no one would notice me. No chance. Kids pointed at me, laughed, and sniggered. The whole school, it seemed, knew about my lunchtime nap and found it funny. Apart from Leah. She was in my Social Studies class, and she sat next to me. That was good of her, particularly since her friends were in a group having a good laugh at my expense. It takes courage to be seen with a loser. She leaned toward me.

"Bloody hell, Michael," she whispered. "You don't exactly help yourself, do you? I mean, falling asleep at lunchtime!"

"Yeah, well . . ."

"I didn't find out about it until last lesson. I don't want you to think that I'd have left you there if I'd known."

"I don't think you'd have done that."

"What's this I heard about a note pinned on you?"

"Nothing. No big deal."

"Yeah, well, if I find out who did it . . ."

We didn't finish. The Social Studies teacher suddenly slammed his fist down on the desk.

"There seems to be an unnecessary amount of noise in this classroom today. School has not finished yet, so I suggest you get your textbooks out and turn to page thirty-five. The ecology of the Murray River system. Right . . ."

• • •

When the bell rang, I stayed behind to ask about our homework, but only because I didn't want to leave with the rest of the students. The teacher answered patiently, even though he had already clearly explained the assignment. When I thought most students would have left the building, I thanked him and gathered up my books. Leah was waiting for me in the corridor.

"Getting the bus, Michael?"

Normally, I would have been pleased to walk with her. I was touched she had waited for me. But I had business to attend to.

"Thanks, Leah, but I've got something to do. I'll get the bus later."

After she'd gone, I waited in the corridor for a minute and then left the school grounds by a side entrance. A few kids were hanging around, but they didn't bother me. Down the road, I found a bench to sit on and waited. I had a clear view of the school. I needed to check something. It was crazy. It was impossible. But my heart wouldn't stop hammering.

After twenty minutes, the stooped figure of Mr. Atkins appeared at the main entrance. He walked straight past the staff car park and left the grounds by a side gate. This was a bonus. I had expected him to get in a car. A license plate was all I had hoped for. I waited until he was some way down the road and then followed. If he turned around, he'd spot me. Someone of my size is difficult to miss. Mr. Atkins, though, seemed deep in thought. I stayed as close as I could.

It was madness. What happens in the Dream is the product of my brain waves. It has nothing to do with the outside world, the real world. But the visit to Mrs. Atkins had been strange. It wasn't just the way the dog seemed to sense me. It wasn't even that I couldn't fully control Mrs. Atkins's reactions. I patted my pocket, and I almost hoped I would find that Mrs. Atkins wouldn't bear any resemblance to my creation. Mr. Atkins probably didn't even have a dog. But I couldn't still the rush of excitement in my blood.

Mr. Atkins took a totally different route than the one I had followed at lunchtime. I suppose he might have been heading somewhere other than home, but it didn't seem likely to me. After twenty minutes, he turned into the drive of an elevated house on a quiet street. This took me by surprise, but I quickened my steps and was across the street and watching as he went in the front door. I sat down on the grass for a few moments. I was sweating from the walk, and my legs felt rubbery. I waited until my heart stopped hammering. Then I started a slow walk back to the bus stop. I needed to think.

Mr. Atkins did have a dog. It jumped up at him as he searched for his house keys. It wasn't the dog in the Dream. The real dog was brown, rather than black, but it was about the same size and roughly the same breed. But the main thing that bothered me was Mrs. Atkins. She opened the door while Mr. Atkins was fumbling with his keys and trying to stop the dog from jumping.

I saw her for only a few moments. But she was the twin of the person in the Dream. Her hair was the same, her tired, shuffling walk the same. Only the clothes were different. Maybe the dog and Mrs. Atkins could have been dismissed as coincidence. Even the glimpse I caught of her eyes as she leaned to kiss her husband on the cheek could have been argued away. Even though I'm good with eyes and would have sworn they were the same.

The clinching thing was the bulge in the pocket of my shirt. A lump of sugar. How did it get there? I popped it into my mouth and felt the sweetness crumble on my tongue. It tasted like proof.

When I got home, Dad was still at work. Mary opened the door and gave me a big hug.

"Hey, you," she said. "Guess what? You've had a visitor. Someone from school."

My mind was still swimming with the possibilities of sugar. Even so, my heart skipped a beat.

"Leah?" I said. "Short girl, with hair that curls under her chin?"

Mary laughed.

"In your dreams, mate," she said. "No, this was a boy. Said his name was Martin. You've only missed him by ten minutes."

4.

"He was charming, that Martin. Said he was a friend of yours."

She put the slightest stress on the word *friend.* I almost couldn't bear it. Mary had waited so long for this. It was there in her eyes. Planning my social life. Sleepovers with Martin, going to watch football with Martin, long phone calls with Martin, playing computer games with Martin. I felt weak before her naked hope.

"Said he'd met you at school and wanted to check if you were settling in. Isn't that kind of him? Said he was worried you might find some of the kids unfriendly. He was so disappointed you weren't here. Oh, and he left a message. He'll probably see you on the bus tomorrow, and he wanted to know what costume you'd be wearing to the Social on Friday—and if the two of you could go to the Social together."

I knew I was in trouble.

"What's the Social, Michael?" she said over the rim of her teacup.

"Oh, it's like a school party," I said, trying to sound casual. It wouldn't work. I knew Mary too well.

"Brilliant!" she said. "For the whole school?"

"Just the Year Tens."

"And what did Martin mean about a costume? Is it a costume party?"

"Sort of. It's got a theme."

Mary was getting more excited by the minute.

"I used to love costume parties," she said. "What's the theme?"

"Horror."

"Well, we are going to have to get busy. It's what, Tuesday now. If I'm going to make something, we'll have to decide tonight what you are going as. I could pick up material tomorrow."

"Listen, Mary. I'm not sure I want to go."

She put her cup down and the saucer rattled. This could get unpleasant.

"What do you mean?"

"I'm not sure about it, that's all."

She just frowned at me until I turned my head away. I felt her hand on my wrist but kept my head down.

"Michael," she said. "We need to talk."

"I know what you are going to say, Mary."

She snorted. "Good. It won't come as any surprise to you, then. Listen, Michael. If you're determined not to go, I can't force you, and neither can your dad. You're too old for that now. But you owe me a hearing at least. Is that too much to ask?"

How could I say yes? It was impossible. Mary plucked nervously at her bottom lip, flipped open a pack of cigarettes, and went to light one.

"Dad'll go mad," I said. "You know he hates the smell."

And Dad would smell it, even hours later. He blamed me, never Mary, so I didn't like it when she smoked in the house.

"Oh, just the one," she said. "I'll open the back door and let some air in. He won't smell it."

I didn't say anything. She sat for a moment blowing out a determined stream of smoke.

"Michael," she said finally. "You've been to seven schools in four years. It's no wonder you don't make friends. Now, I know it's not your fault. I know that every school you've been to has been a nightmare, that you've been bullied, emotionally and physically, at all of them. I can only begin to imagine what that must be like. And I worry about you, Michael. I worry about you so much."

Her eyes brimmed with tears. It wrenched something inside me. I covered her hand with mine. I could feel it trembling. Mary took another drag on the cigarette. Ash fell to the floor.

"This is a chance, Michael. That's all. A chance for a little happiness. You've been invited to the Social by a boy from school. The first time I can remember anyone inviting you anywhere. Don't blow it, Michael. Take a chance. Please. If not for your sake, then for mine."

And that's how it was decided. A series of images flashed into my mind. The first time I saw Mary, standing on the doorstep, about two years after Mum died. She carried a nervous smile and a canvas bag. Mary sitting on the side of my bed, murmuring nonsense and wiping my tears away. Mary plucking at her bottom lip and smoking, always smoking. Her laugh, the way her mouth turned down when she disapproved, her ability to put up with pain and loneliness. I knew all about that. Mary loved me. She held nothing back. And I loved her. Sometimes it's that simple.

"All right, Mary," I said. "I'll go."

"Really?"

"Sure. It might be fun." I could always find a quiet spot somewhere and sit out a couple of hours. It wasn't like I was really giving anything up.

"Oh, Michael!" She clapped her hands together, like a little kid. It made me laugh. "That's brilliant. It really is. You'll have such a good time."

She leapt to her feet and started opening drawers in the kitchen cabinet.

"Pen. Paper. We need to brainstorm ideas for your costume. Damn it, I know there's a pen here somewhere."

I watched as she rushed around. She reminded me of Mum sometimes, particularly around the eyes. Not that I could remember much of Mum, but I've got photographs. Mary's hair was getting grayer, and lines were deepening on her face. But her eyes were clear and sparkling. It was difficult not to get caught up in her enthusiasm. I found myself rummaging around in my schoolbag for my pencil case while she gabbled on.

"What about a zombie? Too obvious? Perhaps it should be something no one else will wear. Like . . . oh, I don't know. A creature from outer space? I could do you all green. Hey, what about the Incredible Hulk?"

"I'm the size for it. I could go as the Incredible Bulk."

Normally, she would give me hell if I made jokes about myself, but now she just laughed, took my pen and an exercise book, and started scribbling.

Dad rang. He told me he was working overtime and he'd drop in at the pub afterward. I'd have to cook for myself, and I shouldn't wait up. He didn't mention Mary, but I passed the message on. She smiled.

"Not the first time we'll have taken care of ourselves, Michael. Anyway, we've plenty of planning to do. And I can afford to have another ciggie. Or two."

She triumphantly produced another smoke from her pack and lit up. I didn't have the heart to complain.

I went to bed early. We hadn't made much progress on a costume, but we'd kicked ideas about. Anyway, I knew Mary. She'd rush around, but I'd still have to get something at the last minute. I left her roughing out designs. They seemed very complicated to me, but she was happy. She gave me a big hug and dropped ash on my shoulder.

"Sleep well, Michael," she said. "You know, I've a feeling things are starting to change for you. New place, new school, new friends. It's all coming together."

I didn't want to tell her that from where I was standing it all seemed on the point of unraveling.

I thought about it when I got to bed. Why had Martin Leechy come to my house? What was in it for him? Maybe it was just excitement, the risk of entering enemy territory. Perhaps he wanted me to understand that nowhere was safe, not even my own home. I couldn't tell. All I could really be sure of was that he was dangerous, even more so than Jamie. Because Martin was unpredictable.

Sooner or later, one of them would get me. That was certain.

I put it out of my mind. There was no point worrying about the inevitable. And anyway, I wanted to focus on sugar lumps; a tired, sick woman; and the nature of the Dream. I tried to think it through carefully, but an image kept getting in the way. From a math lesson, in some school I had now forgotten. The teacher, I remember, had made us cut a strip of paper, half a meter long. Then we had to staple the ends together, forming a band. The thing was, we had to twist one end over before we stapled. The band had a kink in it. And it was so cool. He'd made us draw a line along the surface, and it joined both planes. It just kept going round and round. I even remember what it was called. A Möbius strip. I kept the picture in my head while I explored my logic.

I had visited a woman in the Dream. In the real world I had seen a woman who was identical. Coincidence? The logical explanation was that I might have seen her before, in the real world, and attached her to my Dream vision. The imagination needs something to build on.

In the Dream, she and the dog had behaved in ways I couldn't fully control. Circumstantial evidence? That happened sometimes. It used to happen all the time before my control got better. Why should I think I'd got it exactly right?

A lump of sugar I had put into my pocket in the Dream. A lump that was still there when I woke on the oval. A dream sweetness that melted on my real tongue. Proof? I couldn't think past that.

What if the real world was one side of a Möbius strip and the Dream the other? What if a twist made two separate places one connected plane I could travel along? Wouldn't that mean I could remove a tumor in the Dream and it would be removed in the real world? The first tingling sense of possibility ran through me as I drifted toward sleep. My head was full of sugar, knots of cancer, and curved strips of paper.

Dad came in late. I jerked upright in bed at the sound of his stamping. I knew he was drunk. I could read the signs. The way the fridge door slammed, the way cups and plates rattled. After a few minutes, I heard his feet along the corridor. My door crashed open, and a wedge of light fell across my face.

Dad stood there, swaying slightly.

"You've been smoking again," he said. There was darkness in his eyes. "The whole place stinks of it."

"I haven't, Dad. Honest."

He looked at me a little longer.

"You're a lying bastard," he said. "The kitchen reeks of smoke. I can smell it on you from here. Get up and get changed."

"Dad. No. Please."

He slammed the door. I lay for a few moments longer, but I had no choice. I swung my legs out of bed and found the shorts, bright red and shiny, at the bottom of my chest of drawers. I pulled them up and the waistband dug into my gut. Even so, the fabric flapped below my knees. In the wardrobe mirror, flabby breasts flopped, pale and hairless. My stomach fell in folds over the white waistband. Only my legs were thin. I swallowed against an upsurge of bile.

The back door in the kitchen was open and I went outside. Dad was waiting. He wore blue satin shorts and jigged on his toes. A fluorescent light on the outside wall destroyed the night. He handed me the gloves and I put them on.

"Left foot toward me, pointing at the target," he said. "Knees bent. Not that much. Find your balance, so you can go forward or backward. Left hand up, just below the eye. Forearm's your best defense, remember. Elbow down to protect the gut. Side on. Make yourself small. Right arm higher, son. Where does the power come from, Michael?"

"The shoulder, Dad."

"That's right. The shoulder. Get weight behind it. And what's the golden rule?"

"Movement, Dad."

"Movement. Jab and dance away. Keep moving. It's difficult to hit a moving target, son. Remember the legs and the eyes. Watch your opponent at all times. Keep moving at all times."

He snaked out a jab. It caught me just above the temple.

"You're not watching and you're not moving. You should have seen that coming. Improve your reflexes."

He moved closer, ducked his left shoulder, and brought his right fist through into my stomach. I felt the rush of air leave me.

"The sucker punch," he said. "You fall for it every time. Watch my eyes, son. It's all in the eyes. Come on. Free-hit time. Give it your best shot."

He dropped his gloves slightly, dancing lightly on his toes. I moved toward him and he skipped away. Sweat was stinging my eyes and my stomach hurt. I tried to move quicker, and he circled around me, dropping his arms to his side. I brought my right arm over, and he swayed out of the way. I stumbled and he cuffed me on the back of the head.

"Balance, son. Keep up on your toes and never lose the balance."

Afterward, he slung an arm around my neck. His mood had improved. He smelled of sweat and beer.

Mary came into my bedroom later. I was staring at the ceiling. She sat on the edge of my bed, brushed my hair back from my face, and kissed me on the forehead. We didn't say anything. But I thought about how the real world might be different. Maybe, with a twist, two worlds would join. If I could do that, it would change everything.

And then . . . Well, people had better watch out.

Wednesday

1.

I dream of Mum.

We are on a beach. I'm building sand castles, and the sun is reflecting off the waves. Little shards of light, like splinters, hurt my eyes. Mum is lying on her back on an orange towel. Dad is wading out of the surf. I squint against the sun. He is a dark cutout, impossibly thin, diamond flashes of light on his silhouette. Mum gets up, pushes hair away from my eyes, and smiles at me. My sun hat is tight at my temples, loose and floppy across my shoulders. My hands are small and pudgy. They fuss with the wall of a castle, patting crumbling sand into place. Mum rubs cold, oily sunscreen into my back, but my attention is fixed on the castle. It's falling apart.

I know I'm dreaming but do nothing to alter it. Not when I dream of Mum. I feel her hands across my skin, and I feel the texture of the sand. The sun is a tingle on my bare legs, the sound of the surf a heartbeat. Dad throws himself down next to us. Another castle slips and slides, and he cups it in his hands, smoothing it. He grins at me, but I frown back. He's not doing it right.

Mum calls to me from a distance and I look up. She is in a car, and the sound of the waves is building. The rhythm gets faster, so the pulse becomes a throbbing roar. Dad has gone. I see Mum through the windshield. She seems asleep. Her face is very pale. There is a ticking sound and colors flare. I am aware of a pain in my left leg. I want to run, but something picks me up and the world turns dark.

I sat up, my heart thumping. No glass this time. That only happens when I Dreamride. Through the curtains, the first glow of dawn washed my bedroom in pastels. I waited as my breathing slowed and felt the pain in my leg. My left leg. Sharp—as though I had been stabbed. The pain swelled. I threw back the covers and examined my pasty flesh. Nothing. Not even a bruise. But the pain felt real.

I swung myself out of bed, hobbled to the bathroom, and turned on the shower. As the cold water sprayed over me, the pain faded. By the time I toweled myself dry, it had become a dull ache. I sat on the toilet and tried to make sense of the buzzing in my head.

Maybe I was going mad. A Möbius strip! Just a scientific curiosity, something to amuse schoolkids. What next? Wormholes in space, stupid theories about the curvature of time, parallel dimensions? I needed to keep a grip on reality. Yet I could still taste the sugar on my tongue and feel the twinge in my leg. I knew I wouldn't be able to stop thinking about twisted planes, but another school day awaited. I had to deal with that.

Mary wasn't in the kitchen, but the door was ajar. I knew I would find her in the garden. Sure enough, she was behind her favorite palm tree, having a smoke. She jumped when I snuck up on her.

"God, Michael," she said. "I thought you were your dad!"

"You should give up," I said.

She took another drag.

"Your dad or cigarettes?" she said.

She was red around the eyes.

"Are you all right, Mary?" I asked.

She flicked the butt into the undergrowth and rubbed at her face. "Oh, take no notice of me," she said with a weak smile. "I didn't sleep well, that's all."

I knew why. Waiting until I had gone to sleep, going back to her bedroom, harsh words whispered, insults from Dad, lying in the darkness wondering how to get through another night, another day. Possibilities can be scary at times.

"Listen, love," she said. "I don't feel so hot this morning. Can you make your own breakfast? I just want to stay in the fresh air."

"Smoking cigarettes?"

"So shoot me," she said.

"No problem," I said. "The breakfast, that is. Not the shooting. And I'll bring you a cup of tea."

"You're a good boy, Michael."

I made myself a couple of rounds of toast. Plenty of butter, so the rounds were heavy and yellow. Dad wouldn't be up for a while. He'd need to sleep off the grog. I risked a third slice and took a cup of tea out to Mary. She hadn't moved.

"You're a lifesaver," she said.

"You're not going to leave, are you?" I said. The words came out in a rush. "I wouldn't blame you if you did, though." My legs were trembling. I couldn't bear it if she left. I couldn't bear knowing it was my fault.

Mary snapped her head up. She spilled some of her tea. "Michael! What makes you ask such a question? Of course I'm not going to leave." She put her cup on the ground and her arms around me. "What nonsense you talk sometimes. You are the dearest thing in the world to me. As long as you want me here, I'll be here. Okay?"

I nodded, but the possibility was fixed in my head. The fear that one day I'd get up, find a note, an empty kitchen, and the smell of cigarette smoke fading into nothing. Like Mum's perfume. I used to smell it everywhere. Now I can't remember it at all. Everything fades in time. All I had was Mary and the Dream. I couldn't cope with losing either one. I wanted to tell her that, but it didn't seem fair.

"I'd better get off to school," I said.

She smoothed my hair from my eyes, even though it didn't need it. For a moment I thought she was going to say something else, but she just sighed and nodded.

"Mikey, I'm so sorry, but I haven't done a packed lunch," she said. "Listen, take a ten from the pot. Get yourself something from the school canteen."

There was a pot on a shelf in the kitchen. Once a week, Dad put money in it for groceries. I put receipts from the supermarket back in it, with any change. He balanced the accounts on Sunday.

"He'll know," I said.

"Not until Sunday," she replied. "Even then, you can always say you lost a receipt or something. That happens."

It had. Twice. And I'd had to get all the groceries out, and Dad and I had gone through them, writing estimated prices down on a piece of paper until the shortfall in the pot had been accounted for. So I knew he'd find out this time. But the thought of chicken satays or a burger and chips was powerful. Maybe I could find a receipt in the rubbish bin at the supermarket that added up to ten dollars. Maybe he wouldn't look too closely at the items on it.

He'd find out. But it would be worth it. While I was eating, that is. I took sixty from the pot. I had to pick up some groceries on my way home anyway.

The walk to the bus stop got rid of the last of the pain in my leg. It was going to be a hot day. The sun was pale and watery through the trees, and the mist on the horizon was burning off. Within hours, the sun would be fierce and the humidity would climb. Already I could feel damp in my armpits.

Nothing happened on the bus ride. Leah didn't get on. Martin didn't get on. Every time the bus stopped, I watched the queue of kids out of the corner of my eye. I didn't relax until the aisle of the bus filled with jostling bodies and the school came into view. I waited until everyone else got off before I stepped down.

I stood blinking in the sunshine and waited for the crowds to thin. There were so many things going around in my head. Martin Leechy, obviously. Jamie Archer. The Year 10 Social, Leah, and Mary. Most of all, a woman with darkness in her head and a strip of twisted paper. I needed a calm day to sort out my thinking.

It started well. Home Group was quiet. Leah stayed with her

friends, though she hovered around the edges and didn't seem to talk much. A few times I caught her watching me. Mr. Atkins was also deep in his own head, but I couldn't read what he was seeing. He might have been thinking about something at home. It was impossible to tell.

I sat by myself, close to the window, and looked outside. Instinctively, I checked for differences. If two worlds could twist and join—if that was possible—I might be able to see differences appear in reality, as they did in the Dream. I didn't see any, but the exercise calmed me. I almost drifted off, it was so peaceful.

The trouble started in the first lesson.

2.

Math.

I sat at the side of the room while the others found their seats. A knot of boys, the last group to enter the classroom, bustled in. Martin Leechy was among them. I opened my math book and bent my head over it. Even as I did, I knew it wouldn't do any good. He sat next to me, fingers laced together on the desk, staring straight ahead at the teacher. He didn't get any books out.

Mr. Williams, the teacher, took the roll. He didn't read out Martin's name. I could only hope he'd notice a boy who had no business being there and send him on his way. I hoped it wouldn't take too long.

Mr. Williams closed the roll book and stood up. He wrote "Trigonometry: Sines, Cosines, and Tangents" on the whiteboard and turned to face us.

"Game over!" he yelled, and the thrum of conversation dwindled and died. "Thank you." He pointed toward the whiteboard. "The module we are starting today is a tricky little devil. And that means you have to pay attention. What is this module like, Gemma Watkins?"

"A tricky little devil, sir."

"Spot on. Now, you must ask if you don't understand. I do not mind explaining things ten times, if necessary. Actually, that's a lie. But it is better than having to explain later, when it becomes clear you did not pay attention the first time around. Capisce?"

Martin leaned toward me.

"Thinks he's cool, doesn't he?" he whispered. I didn't react.

"Cool," continued Mr. Williams. "We are on the same wavelength. Okay, exercise books out . . . yes, that means you . . . and copy down the heading on the board. Quick, guys."

For about five minutes, Martin was quiet. He still hadn't got a book out. He sat staring straight ahead, chin in hands, while Mr. Williams explained about trigonometry. The only sound in the class was the scratch of pen on paper as we took notes. Martin cupped his hands around his mouth and leaned toward me again.

"Decided on your costume for the Social yet?" he said. I ignored him. He poked me in the ribs with a finger.

"I'm talking to you, Michael. Don't ignore me."

I put my head down and kept quiet. He poked me in the ribs again, harder this time.

"Whoa. It's not a good idea to ignore me, Mikey. I don't like being ignored. It hurts my feelings. You wouldn't like me when my feelings have been hurt."

"Please," I hissed.

Mr. Williams stopped pacing and glared at us. He stood for a moment and then continued talking, punctuating his explanations with notes on the board.

"Please, what?" said Martin a minute later. "What do you please want me to do? I can't please you if I don't know what you want."

I ignored him and he jabbed me in the ribs again. It really hurt this time. I had to choke back a gasp of pain. I glanced up and Mr. Williams was writing on the board, his back turned nearly all the way round from us. I had to take the risk.

"Later," I said as quietly as I could. "I'll talk to you later."

There was a giggle from the back of the class, and Mr. Williams spun to face us. He looked directly at me.

"Michael, isn't it?"

I nodded. He wrote my name carefully in the top right corner of the whiteboard and then turned to smile at me.

"Michael, you are new here and maybe you don't understand the rules of the game. Just to let you know, in my class, you are quiet while I'm teaching. That way we all have the chance to learn. First warning and your name goes up here." He pointed to the whiteboard. "Second time and you're history. Capisce?"

Another giggle started but was instantly cut off as the teacher's gaze snapped on someone behind me.

"Yes, sir. Sorry, sir," I said.

Mr. Williams smiled and turned back to the board. He wrote nearly all of an equation before Martin's fist slammed into my side. I couldn't help it. I yelped in pain. Mr. Williams paused, the pen hovering over the board. Then he turned slowly. He was still smiling.

"Well, Michael," he said. "Clearly not that sorry. Unless my math fails me, that is strike two! Collect your bag and wait outside the classroom. We will have words later. Ciao." His smile never wavered.

The class was completely quiet. I could feel all eyes on me as I packed my exercise book and pens away. I squeezed past Martin and headed for the door. Some of the students were grinning as I walked down the aisle, but most kept their heads down. So much for keeping a low profile. First there was the cake in the face, then falling asleep on the oval, and now being thrown out of math class. It was only Wednesday morning. Not even halfway through the first week.

I closed the door behind me. Harsh fluorescent lighting illuminated the long corridor. Classroom doors were shut and everything was quiet, apart from the occasional murmur of voices from one room or another. I stood for a while, my back pressed against the wall of the math room. I checked my watch. There were still forty minutes of the lesson left. I slid down the surface of the wall and sat on the cold tiles. At least I'd got away from Martin. Time for thinking.

I thought about him first. Do something. That's what Mr. Atkins had said about Jamie. It's what Dad said as well. Fight back. They agreed on that, if not on the means. Maybe Dad was right. Maybe the only way to get bullies off my back was to challenge them to fight. I'd get the crap beaten out of me. I had no doubt about that. Of course, in films it wouldn't matter. I'd be fighting back. I wouldn't give up. My opponent would respect me for my guts. At the end of the fight, he'd help me to my feet, put an arm around my shoulder, and say, "Hey, guys, this kid is all right. No one's to mess with him, do you hear?" And then he'd help me clean myself up, and we would become best friends.

Trouble is, I just can't ball my fist and force it into someone's face. Ask someone to eat dog shit and they'd be defeated just by thinking about it. That was me. My whole being shrank from the idea. Kids quickly learned that I couldn't fight back. I might as well have worn a sign saying "Hit Me" on my shirt.

Mr. Atkins's way was with words, and at least I wasn't scared of words. But I still knew I couldn't do it. I had little enough in common with kids my own age. I couldn't talk about stuff like that to adults. Even if I could be sure of getting away with it. Anyone who knows anything about schools knows that.

I kept coming back to a twist in a strip of paper. I killed kids in the Dream. It was easy. And I knew that if I could twist the Dream and the real together, Martin would be sorry he had ever been born. He was number one on my list.

I sat with my legs spread out in front of me, staring at the black and gray flecks in the floor tiles. I didn't hear Leah. One moment I was studying the floor, the next she was sitting next to me, like she had magically appeared.

"You scared me," I said.

"Sorry." She smiled, her eyes sparkling with flecks of brightness, like the patterns in the tiles. I smiled back.

"You were deep in thought," she continued. "Feel like telling me about it? Or explaining why you are sitting outside the math room, rather than sweating over Mr. Williams's trigonometry lesson?"

"I got thrown out."

"Well, duh! I could've worked that out for myself," she said, but she wasn't being nasty. "What for?"

"For not keeping quiet while Martin Leechy was poking me," I explained.

Leah frowned and her eyes, this time, sparked with anger.

"It's so unfair," she said. "The school knows what Martin's like, but they turn a blind eye. He's good at sports, good in lessons. Top of his class most times. Off to university in a couple of years. A credit to Millways. It's easier to pretend his other side doesn't exist. It's only a couple of kids who suffer, after all. And they're not a credit to Millways. It makes me mad."

Leah chewed her bottom lip. And it was right then, watching her face screwed up in frustration, that I made my decision to tell her. To share everything about myself. I immediately felt better. She cared about me. How could I not care about her? It was time to make contact.

"I want to tell you something," I said. "Again."

She laughed. "Again?"

"I've already told you, but you won't remember. I told you in a dream."

Leah gave a small smile and brushed a wave of dark hair out of her eyes.

"You're a strange one, Michael," she said.

"You don't know the half of it," I said. "But you will. If you want. Could we talk after school?"

"Come to my place," she said. "My mum's always telling me to bring friends home. She'd be thrilled."

"Shouldn't you ask first?"

"Nah. Don't worry about it."

We arranged to meet in reception after school. Dad would be on late shift and wouldn't be home until after midnight. I could ring Mary. She had been almost hysterical with excitement when she thought Martin was going to be a friend. I couldn't imagine how she'd react when she heard a girl had invited me to her house.

The bell sounded and the thin noise from the classrooms swelled into a shuffling and scraping of chairs. Leah got to her feet and brushed her skirt down.

"Well. See ya later, then," she said. "I'm looking forward to hearing everything, Michael. Soooo mysterious!" And then she was gone, swept up in a tide as all the doors along the corridor opened and a surge of students flowed out. I tried to catch a last glimpse, but she was lost. I got to my feet too.

Time to face Mr. Williams. I wasn't worried anymore. Not about Martin, not about Mr. Williams. A weight had been lifted from me. Leah was taking a friend home.

3.

At recess I went to the canteen to buy a Mars bar.

Mr. Williams had been reasonable. He told me he had been forced to throw me out. Rules were rules. If he'd made an exception in my case, then other students would have thought it unfair. They'd feel they could break the rules as well. Capisce? I did. And I told him that. It was almost funny. He felt bad. Like he was sorry for me and asking forgiveness. He more or less told me he knew someone else in the class had set me up. I didn't say anything. Just apologized, said it wouldn't happen again. He never stopped smiling.

It was a long queue at the canteen. Mr. Atkins was on duty,

standing about ten meters away. I tried to read his eyes, but he was too far away and the sun was behind him. Anyway, I didn't want to stare. The queue shuffled forward. Jamie Archer must have pushed in. He hadn't been behind me a minute before. Yet his voice over my right shoulder was quiet and unmistakable.

"Feeling good, Wrenbury? Feeling pleased with yourself? Think you're safe 'cause your gay mate is looking out for you?" I didn't turn round. "I'll get you, Wrenbury. Sooner or later, you fat bastard."

I left. I didn't need a Mars bar that badly.

I had to go past Mr. Atkins. I tried to slip by, but people tend to spot someone of my size.

"Michael, my friend. How are you this fine day?"

I didn't have much choice. I stopped, even though I could feel Jamie's gaze on my back.

"Good, Mr. Atkins. How are you?"

"In exceptional fettle. Life doesn't get any better than this, Michael. Standing in the full sun, with the humidity in the low nineties, watching out for violence among the socially and ethically challenged. And do you want to know a secret?" He leaned toward me and whispered, "They even pay me. Can you believe my good fortune?"

"I've decided to go to the Social, Mr. Atkins."

"Have you indeed? That is excellent news, Michael." He looked like he meant it. "I'm sure you'll have a splendid time. See me tomorrow at Home Group and I'll sell you a ticket. Ten dollars. A paltry sum that represents stupendous value in this financially stricken time."

Jamie had bought a carton of iced coffee. He was leaning up against the canteen wall, watching us. I glanced at my watch. Only five minutes of recess left. It was easier to stay where I was.

"Mr. Atkins?" I said. "You're a magician. I know the thing with the coin is only a trick but . . . Well, do you believe in magic? Real magic?" I felt dumb as soon as I asked the question, but Mr. Atkins seemed to consider it seriously.

"Real magic, Michael? Well, I suppose we'd have to be careful with our definitions of *real* and *magic,* would we not? What is your opinion?"

"I believe that what some people think is impossible can happen."

Mr. Atkins scratched his nose.

"Indeed. Imagine if someone from two hundred years ago appeared today. Wouldn't the things we take for granted—the motorcar, electricity, computers, television, to name a few—appear magical to such a time traveler? They would be beyond that person's imaginings. So, too, if we were to go forward a couple of hundred years. What wonders would we witness, what magic beyond our comprehension? Yet, do you know something, Michael? What interests me most is the small magic all around us and unacknowledged."

"Sir?"

"Oh, the occasional line in a Year Nine imaginative essay, a flash of kindness in an otherwise brutalized heart, a shy boy who decides to go to a Year Ten Social. These are wonders in themselves, don't you think?"

He smiled. I couldn't be sure, but it seemed there was less pain behind his eyes. I wondered if he had gone home last night, found magic in a woman's face and voice and eyes. I couldn't ask, but I needed to know badly.

The bell rang and I went to English. There was no trouble in that class or in Social Studies. Small magic, as Mr. Atkins might say. At lunch I went straight to the canteen and bought a burger with the lot—egg, bacon, cheese—and a chocolate milk shake. I ignored the snide comments around me. As soon as I was served, I went off to my tree. I sat at its base, facing the oval. I didn't hear or see Martin until he sat down beside me and pulled out a sandwich. We sat together in silence. Eventually, he finished eating, brushed crumbs from his lap, and leaned back against the tree, his head close to mine. Throughout the conversation, he didn't look at me. Not once.

"So, Michael," he said. "I never got an answer. What are you planning to wear to the Social?"

"I don't know," I replied.

"It's tricky, isn't it? I mean, there are so many obvious costumes. Freddy Krueger, Dracula. But we want to be original, don't we? We are not the kind of people to settle for the clichéd. I'm still thinking it through."

I kept quiet.

Martin brushed a few remaining crumbs from his mouth.

"She's a lovely woman, your stepmum. We had a good chat. She's hoping we can become good mates. Isn't that sad? I don't suppose you've made too many friends in your previous schools, have you?"

"No."

"No, I didn't think so. But you know what? I feel sure we *are* going to be mates. Seriously. I reckon we've got a bond between us. Come on. Be honest. Don't you think there's some truth in that?"

And the strange thing was, I could almost agree with him. I glanced at Martin from the corner of my eyes. Leah was right. He was good-looking and confident, as if aware of the power of his attractiveness and comfortable using it. He was exactly the kind of person I would have liked to be, if you took away his cruelty. Comfortable in his own skin. And there was some similarity between us. No one else might have noticed, but I did. It was as if we were linked in some way. Two sides of Mr. Atkins's coin, two sides of the same material, but completely different.

"You're playing games," I said. "You want to hurt me."

He rubbed his chin.

"Well, I can understand you coming to that conclusion,

Michael. I mean, I have to be honest here. The only interaction we have had so far has been unpleasant for you. I acknowledge that. But who knows about the future? Maybe we'll be like those people you see in the movies. Once we've had a big dustup, fought like animals, we'll become friends. You know, a fight might cement our friendship."

I said nothing and he chuckled.

"The thought's occurred to you, hasn't it, Michael?" he continued. "It's almost like I can read your mind, that we *are* on the same wavelength. Promising for a future friendship, don't you think?"

I said nothing.

"Well, I think so," he continued. "I'm optimistic about our relationship."

He got up and brushed off his pants. He moved a few steps away, then turned toward me for the first time.

"Oh, and by the way, Michael. Don't worry about Jamie Archer. He's a loser. A wannabe tough guy. The scariest thing about him is his lack of originality. You've coped with dropkicks like him, I'm sure. But, if you want, I'll give you a hand. I couldn't bear the idea that, in some way, he'd be detracting attention from me. 'Cause it's all about us, Michael. You know that, don't you? Give it some thought. And just let me know if you need help sorting him out."

He wandered off to a group of boys playing football. In a few moments he had disappeared into the ruck of players. I still had most of my burger left. It was cold and there were globs of congealed grease on the edges. I didn't feel hungry anymore. But I ate it anyway.

During the last lesson of the day, I got a message that Miss Palmer wanted to see me straight after school. I worried about missing Leah. We'd arranged to meet at reception immediately after classes. I could only hope the meeting with Miss Palmer wouldn't take too long and that Leah would wait.

When the bell went, I rushed down to Miss Palmer's office and knocked on the door. She opened it slightly and gave me a quick smile.

"Thanks for coming, Michael. I'll be with you in a few moments. Take a seat, please."

I sat in one of the four chairs against the wall outside her office. I checked my watch. It was ironic. The one day I wanted to get away on time was the one day I couldn't. Normally, I'd be fine about sitting around after school. Time's not important if you haven't got a life.

I didn't have to wait long. After a few minutes, Miss Palmer opened the door and ushered out a couple of adults. They shook her hand and thanked her for her time. I stood up. Miss Palmer waved them down the corridor and then turned to me.

"Michael, I'm sorry to keep you waiting. Please come in."

I stepped into her office and sat in one of the visitors' chairs. It was still warm. Miss Palmer sat behind her desk and studied me carefully. My eyes found the poster over her shoulder.

"Michael. I spoke to Mrs. Bowyer earlier today." She paused as if to check my reaction. I continued staring at the poster. It was advertising a children's help line. I didn't know who Mrs. Bowyer was. I figured Miss Palmer would tell me and she did.

"The assistant principal in your last school in Northern Queensland. I rang her."

I remembered then. A huge woman with a mustache. She was also going bald. You could see a large area of her scalp just above her right ear. The kids gave her heaps about it. She hadn't liked me. She hadn't liked anyone, as far as I could tell. Miss Palmer seemed to expect some reaction, so I shrugged.

"She said some very interesting things about your time at that school, Michael. About bullying and . . . other things. Do you know what I'm talking about?"

I shrugged. Miss Palmer tapped at her teeth with a pencil. It was a habit she had. I read the poster. Miss Palmer leaned back in her chair.

"We need to have a chat, Michael. Particularly after what happened in Mr. Williams's math class today. I've rung your father and arranged a meeting for tomorrow after school. Mr. Atkins, as your Home Group teacher, will attend as well. I thought I'd let you know in advance, so you could think things over. I'm concerned about you, Michael. I want to help. But I also think you need to start talking to us about what's bothering you. Would you be able to do that, Michael?"

I didn't want to shrug again, so I nodded. It was easier than saying anything.

"Good. Well, I'll look forward to seeing you tomorrow, then."

I was glad to get out of there. I almost ran down the corridor to the main reception. Leah saw me and smiled. It lit up her face. We walked out of the school into the bright sunshine. I angled my face to the sky. After the coldness of school, I needed to feel the sun's warmth. There were clouds drifting against the blue. I could see a swirl of kites riding the wind, small smudges against the sky.

Small magic.

4.

We caught the bus to Leah's place, the same bus I'd take to get home. She lived about half the distance from school that I did. We got off and walked for ten minutes. I didn't say much. I was nervous. It was important to me that Leah didn't think I was crazy. But I wasn't sure how to start. As I rehearsed it in my head, it sounded unlikely, almost unhinged. I would have to trust her. Just tell her. Leah seemed to understand my need for quiet. We walked in comfortable silence.

I walked straight past her place. I'd taken about five steps before I realized she was no longer at my side. I stopped. She was halfway up a driveway, grinning at me. I smiled sheepishly and retraced my steps.

Leah's house was exactly the kind of place I had always wanted to live in. It had a wide balcony sweeping around two sides. Palms in pots stood behind decorative railings. The front door had inlaid stained glass. The grass had been freshly mown. It was big and bright and welcoming.

Even before I went in I knew there would be polished wood floors and a kitchen full of light. I could smell baking bread.

Leah noticed me staring.

"What do you think?" she said.

"It's amazing," I said. I meant it too.

"Well, come in and meet Mum. Dad won't be back from work for a few hours."

"Are you sure it's okay?" I asked. "I mean, your mum's not expecting me."

"Don't worry. My friends are always welcome. I told you that."

She took me by the hand and led me around the back. The yard was beautiful. There was a big kidney-shaped swimming pool, and palm trees leaned over it, giving shade. A chatter of lorikeets filled the trees. A small dog appeared and jumped up at me. It was wiry—one of those breeds you either love or hate. I loved them. It skipped around my ankles, twisting its body in excitement, yelping and springing at me. I knelt down and scuffed my hands through the fur of its neck. It froze, its head turned up, bathing in pleasure. Its eyes were pure milk.

"You've made a friend, Michael," said Leah. "That's Scamp. Scamp, this is Michael."

"Is he blind?" I asked.

"Yes," Leah said. "But it doesn't seem to bother you much, does it, mate?" The dog squirmed his way over to Leah. She picked him up and hugged him to her chest. "The vet reckons it's too dangerous to operate on his eyes. Says Scamp's ticker mightn't be up to it."

The back door opened and Leah's mum came out. It had to be Leah's mum. They had the same warm eyes. Even their hair was cut in a similar style. Leah put the dog down, and it yapped around my ankles again.

"Mum, meet Michael Terny," said Leah. "Michael, this is my mum."

I put out my hand and wondered if it was sweaty.

"Pleased to meet you, Mrs. McIntyre," I said.

Her smile was a clone of Leah's.

"Pleased to meet you too, Michael," she said. "But you can forget the Mrs. McIntyre business. Call me Carol."

For a moment I felt dizzy. It was the strangest thing. It stirred old memories. I didn't mean to say anything. It just came out.

"That was my mum's name."

Mrs. McIntyre paused and cocked her head to one side.

"Was?" she asked.

"She's dead," I replied.

"I'm sorry to hear that, Michael." She was too. It was written in her eyes. "Come in and have a drink," she continued. "Are you staying for tea?"

"Well . . ."

"Yes, he is, Mum," said Leah. "He just needs to ring home to let his folks know."

"Well, don't just stand there, girl. Show Michael the phone while I get some lemonade together. Homemade lemonade all right with you, Michael?"

"Yes, Mrs. McIntyre. Thank you."

"Call me Carol, remember?"

Leah took my hand and led me inside. The kitchen was as I imagined it—bright and warm with spotless wooden surfaces. The smell of baking bread made my mouth water. Leah took me into the hall to the phone.

"Come outside when you're done," she said. "We'll have our lemonade by the pool."

I rang Mary and told her I was going to be late. She was so pleased she could barely speak. Two friends, she must have been thinking. Two friends. Like a dream come true. And then she found words. I almost had to hang up on her, she gabbled so much in excitement.

Out in the garden, Mrs. McIntyre was setting a table under a broad sailcloth and Leah was carrying a tray with glasses and a jug of icy lemonade. The dog was scurrying around her legs. Mrs. McIntyre waved me over.

"Come and make yourself comfortable, Michael," she said. "Would you like to go for a swim? I guess you won't have brought any swimmers along, but you can swim in your shorts."

"Thanks, Mrs. McIntyre, but I'll pass on the swim. If I jumped into a pool, I'd drain it."

She reached over and tapped me hard on the head.

"Hello?" she said. "Anyone in there? It's Carol. Does your friend suffer from short-term memory loss, Leah? Anyway, who cares about the pool? I think it can cope with you, Michael."

I smiled. "Thanks anyway, Mrs. . . . . Carol, but I won't today. Maybe some other time."

"Right. Your choice. Now, you'll have to excuse me. I've got about ten things on the go in the kitchen, and if I don't get back to them, we'll be eating charcoal tonight. Just shout if you need anything. Better still, bring out some snacks and dips, Leah. Tide you guys over until tea."

She disappeared back into the house. Leah and I sat in silence. Scamp jumped up on her lap and slobbered at her neck, making her giggle. After a while, he settled down and curled into a shaggy ball, his head hanging over the side of her legs. With an outsized sigh, he closed his eyes and fell asleep. I stretched back in my chair and looked around the garden.

The afternoon sun dappled the pool. Little waves of light

reflected up from the water's surface and made the fronds on the palms shimmer with gold and yellow. Tiny birds dipped in flight and brushed the water, sending more ripples across the pool. Everything danced in light. I reached for my lemonade. Even that seemed perfect, the way the beads of moisture glistened on the glass. I pressed it to my forehead and shivered at the chill. I almost didn't want to drink. I didn't want to alter anything. Maybe Leah felt that too. We listened to the chatter of the birds, bathed in the sun's reflection, and said nothing. When I finally took a long drink of lemonade, I had never tasted anything so good.

I knew Leah was waiting for me to start. But the words I had rehearsed now seemed stupid. Instinctively, I checked for differences. This world was like a dream. I couldn't be sure I wouldn't suddenly wake in a dark and comfortless bedroom. But differences were all around. The air was alive with change, the shadows and patterns of light always moving. I gave up. Sometimes you have to trust.

"Leah," I said. "I want to tell you some things I've never told anyone else. But . . ."

"But you're afraid I won't understand, or I'll think it's stupid. That I'll show you, in some way, that you were wrong to trust me. And, if that happens, you'll feel more alone than you do now." Leah kept her gaze fixed in the distance, beyond the palms. She stroked Scamp's head.

"Mum died when I was six."

I hadn't meant to talk about that. I was going to talk about the Dream. But the words just came out. Now that they'd started, I let them carry on. "She was killed by a drunk driver. Hit her car head-on. Mum was trapped in the car. She . . . she died. I don't remember much about it. The other guy. He was all right. Hardly a scratch."

I remembered some things. I remembered Dad and me in a courtroom about a year later. I remembered the guy being hugged by his friends and family. I hadn't known what was happening, but I could remember the expression on Dad's face. It was as though his life simply drained away at that moment. The guy got off on a technicality—something to do with the blood tests the police had done. All I knew was the person who'd killed my mum was free, surrounded by love. Not a scratch.

"Dad started drinking. He couldn't work. He couldn't sleep. He couldn't stay still for any time at all."

But that didn't tell the whole tale. How can you describe watching your father curl into a brittle and dry husk, moving from place to place in search of something always out of reach? How can you explain about a seven-year-old boy, fat and unhappy, cleaning vomit from a bedroom floor while his dad howled at the ceiling or, worse, just stared at the walls, unseeing, unresponsive?

"We traveled. Dad would suddenly pack up our things, stick

them in the truck, and we'd take off." To dusty, flyblown settlements with parched earth and a single pub, or cities where everyone moved with purpose. Except us.

"He'd find a job. I'd go to school. But it wouldn't last." Because sooner or later, there would be a fight, or Dad would crawl into the bottom of a bottle and stay there. "We'd move on. Dad got thinner and thinner. I got fatter." How predictable. It was almost shameful to talk about it. Dad's prop was grog, and mine was food. We were two walking clichés. "And school got worse and worse."

I glanced over at Leah. She hadn't moved, but her eyes glistened. I sucked in a deep breath and continued.

"And then Mary, my stepmum, came along. Literally appeared, standing on the doorstep, smiling at me. Dad hadn't mentioned her. He'd stopped talking to me by then. He was at work when she turned up." I smiled as I remembered. "She came in, made herself a cup of tea, the first of thousands, and we sat and talked for hours. Mary told me she was here to stay, that I could rely on her." I didn't believe her, of course. Not then and not for a long time. I didn't want another mum. Anyway, I figured she'd never be able to put up with Dad and me. I was shocked that Dad had even tried for another relationship. He was only happy in the company of Jim Beam or Johnnie Walker.

"But she stayed. And school was bearable because she stayed. It took a long time for me to believe she wouldn't leave. At times

I still can't believe it. Now I know that without her, I wouldn't . . . I don't know. I don't think I could go on. There are two things in my life that are precious. One is Mary. The other is the Dream."

I laughed. "That was what I wanted to tell you about. The Dream. The rest of this stuff . . . I don't know. I didn't mean to talk about it. Sorry."

I finished my lemonade. My throat was dry. I couldn't remember the last time I had talked so much.

"Have you heard of lucid dreaming, Leah?" I asked.

Leah frowned. "I know what *lucid* means," she said. "It means 'clear' or 'well-spoken.' I've no idea what it has to do with dreaming."

So I explained again. And while I did, I thought back to the very beginnings of the Dream. After Mum died, my dreams became more and more vivid. Some were nightmares, sure. But other dreams, ordinary dreams, as well. I would wake five or six times in the night, bathed in sweat, images burned on my mind. I'd fall back asleep and the dreams would take up right where they'd left off. It was as if they were calling to me in some way.

Riding the Dream came shortly after. I had a particularly vivid and recurring dream. I was in school, standing on the oval surrounded by four boys. I couldn't get away. I had to stand while they baited me, faces twisted in hatred. Five nights of the same dream, before I spotted the first difference. It was small—

I think a shirt changed color—and then other differences flooded in. The way the sun shone, the color of the grass, the sounds and smells. This time I didn't wake up. I stayed asleep. And rode the Dream.

I didn't tell Leah what I did to the boys in the Dream. But I did mention the glass—how I encountered it on the way back to the real world. She'd hardly said anything throughout my explanation. I couldn't see her eyes, and I was desperate to know if there was understanding or contempt or pity in them. I hesitated. But it was too late. I'd come this far. I might as well finish the journey.

"Now . . . oh God. This sounds crazy. I know it sounds crazy. I think I might have found a way for things in the Dream to affect the real world." I told her about my visit to Mr. Atkins's house. I described what I found, what I did. I told her about the cube of sugar. I babbled, eager to get it over and done with. When I finished, there was silence. Even the chattering of birds was muted. Sweat beaded on my forehead, and I reached out to refill my glass. My hand was shaking.

"I know this sounds stupid," I said finally. "I'm sorry if—"

"We need to find a way to test it," Leah said.

I stared at her. Her eyes were bright and fixed on mine.

"What?" I said.

"This link between the Dream and the real world. We need to test if it's really there. Or if you've dreamed it all. That's right, isn't it?"

"You mean you believe me?"

Annoyance flashed briefly across her face.

"Of course I believe you. Why shouldn't I?" She ruffled Scamp's fur. "Now just shut up a moment, Michael. I think you've done quite enough talking. I need to think. You can do what you like in the Dream, go anywhere, do anything. And you're in control. So we need to devise a test. When you dream tonight, you could do something specific. Something that changes the real world in a way we can check. That can't be beyond us."

She smiled.

"What?" I said.

"Let's see if you can work a simple miracle tonight, Michael. Then we'll know, one way or another." She hugged the dog to her chest.

5.

The supermarket was ugly. Big cream tiles made it look like a public toilet block. Inside, the aisles were narrow and crowded with boxes. The fluorescent lighting flickered.

I hadn't made a list, but I knew we needed bread, milk, and eggs. There were other things, but I reckoned I'd see them as I wandered down the aisles. I liked shopping. I liked to take my time in each aisle, examining the shelves. There's always interesting stuff. Tins of Asian vegetables, shrink-wrapped cheese from Norway, CDs, DVDs, choker chains for dogs. Sometimes I imagined the lives of people who bought these things. Homesick people or old people who lived in apartments with only a dog and memories. So many lives out there, closed to me. I liked unfamiliar supermarkets in particular. Because I didn't know the layout, I had to go down every aisle. I got to see everything.

I found the free-range eggs. The first carton had a cracked egg in it. The second carton seemed okay. I took out each egg in turn, felt its cool hardness in my hands, replaced it carefully. There was a flicker of red at the end of the aisle, but by the time I registered that it was there, it had gone. They didn't have music in this supermarket. I liked that. I liked the sounds of shopping carts rolling, the faint burr of the air-conditioning. I got jam as well. Strawberry. Dad liked it on his toast sometimes. Shower gel, the cheapest brand, and toilet paper. I got a good brand. Dad was fussy. Said it was false economy to get the cheap stuff. He didn't want his fingers to go right through it. That didn't apply to shower gel, though. It was really important to remember the rules. I didn't make mistakes anymore.

I browsed the deli. Fresh fish is great. So are green prawns with lumps of ice around them. We get frozen fish fillets in bread crumbs. They don't taste of much, but they are easy to cook, and they keep forever in the freezer. This time the flash of red lingered. I saw it disappear round the end of the frozen-food aisle. My heart beat a little faster. I studied a tray of feta cheese and tried to concentrate on my peripheral vision. But I didn't see it again.

"Can I help you?" The woman had a plastic cap on. For hygiene, I supposed.

"A kilo of barramundi, please."

It came to over a kilo, but I said that was okay. Then I chose a large red emperor. The fish was whole and its eyes were still bright. Over forty dollars' worth of seafood. The waxy white paper felt good in my hands. I put the packages into my basket and went to the milk section. It was opposite the frozen-food section, but the row was deserted. I got three liters of skim. The bakery was close to the checkouts. Halfway there, I glanced to my left. The central aisle stretched to the far end of the supermarket. I saw a tennis shoe, scuffed, disappearing a few rows down. Just the heel. I looked at the breads. There was some terrific focaccia. I picked up two with black olives and mushrooms. I also got three loaves of white sliced, generic supermarket brand. Flavorless but cheap.

I went down the cleaning products aisle. I tucked the focaccia and the waxy white parcels under a shelf of dishwashing liquid. I liked the feel of them in my hand. When I'd finished, you couldn't tell they were there.

I knew Jamie was around. Somewhere. But I didn't see him, not properly. Just the odd flash of red hair, a red shoe disappearing down an aisle.

At the checkout I took the milk out of the cart last. If you take the milk out first, you get a smudge of condensation along the rubber mat and the rest of your groceries get wet.

I know about these things.

6.

I put the groceries away and the receipt and change into the pot on the shelf. It was five-thirty. I'd found another receipt in the rubbish bin outside the supermarket. For eight dollars something. Probably not a good idea, but I put it in the pot anyway. It would almost balance.

Mary was jumping around as I did this. She wanted to know everything that had happened at Leah's. She made me sit at the kitchen table and go through every detail. If I skipped the most insignificant thing, I'd have to stop and start again. She quizzed me on the color of the house, whether the kitchen was tiled, the way the potatoes were cooked. It was exhausting. Her eyes were wide, and she kept clutching at my arm. It was as if we were sharing a movie. I almost laughed. But she was deadly serious. She hardly left the house. Everything that was important to her was filtered through me. I felt responsible. So I told her everything in as much detail as I could. When I'd finished, she leaned back in her chair, sighed, and pulled out a pack of cigarettes. I opened the back door.

Mary's hands were trembling as she lit her cigarette.

"Phew," she said, sucking the smoke down deep. "They sound like a wonderful family, Michael. So does this mean that you and Leah are . . . you know . . . I mean . . ."

I smiled. Not just at Mary's stuttering, but because it was such a perfect reflection of my own feelings. Did this mean that Leah and I were . . . you know? I didn't know. I didn't want to think about it too much.

"We're friends, Mary," I said. "I guess I can say that much." And the words sounded good.

"I'm so happy for you," she said. "And when am I going to meet her? Maybe you could invite her round for tea one day." Panic instantly crossed her face as she considered the disarray in the kitchen. "You'd have to give me plenty of notice. I'd need to get the place cleaned up. The house certainly needs it. What sort of food does she like? I'm not sure if I could do anything complicated. I wouldn't want her to think that we were slobs or unsophisticated. There's a good cookbook around here somewhere. Where did I put it?"

And she was off, rummaging around in drawers as if Leah and her family were due at any moment. I got up and put my arms around her.

"I love you, Mary," I said.

"I love you too, sweetie," she said. "It's got to be around here somewhere. I can't remember the last time I used it, but I do remember unpacking it. Maybe it's still in that crate in the laundry."

I led her back to the kitchen table and eased her into a chair.

"Calm down," I said. "I'll invite her, okay? But don't worry, she's not the sort of person to worry about recipes or a few cobwebs."

Mary leaned forward and grabbed me by the arm.

"Oh, Michael," she said. "Things are changing for you. You deserve it. You really do. You've waited so long. . . ."

Her eyes welled up with tears. She lit another cigarette from the butt of the last and blinked through the smoke. I changed the subject.

"How's the costume going?"

There was material scattered around the kitchen. An ancient sewing machine was on one end of the kitchen table. A black garbage bag, crammed with old clothes, was overflowing onto the floor. When Mary got stuck into a project, she didn't hold back. She would have been working on it all day. But I knew she'd never complete it without my help. It was just the way she was. Lots of energy, but she never finished anything. I'd probably have to rent a costume at the last minute. Not that I was going to tell her that.

"I've got a few ideas, Michael." Her face was bright. "I started on something but then had a rethink. The key is to have a costume that no one else would even consider. So I discarded all the obvious options. Then I got to thinking that possibly . . ."

She gabbled on and I just sat there and held her hand.

What is given can also be taken away. I've learned that. And then you're worse off than if you'd never had it in the first place. So I held on to Mary and half listened as she poured out her ideas. I held on, like she was the one piece of wreckage in a cold and lonely sea. If I let go, I would drown.

I couldn't get to sleep. The night was hot and humid, and I was covered in a thin film of sweat. The fan didn't make a difference. It just moved the stifling air around. I kicked off the top sheet and struggled to find a comfortable position. The pillows seemed leaden and wet where my face touched them. Little sounds around the house were magnified. The creaking of the tin roof as it contracted slightly under the night's relative coolness. The tutting of geckos. The distant howl of a dog.

Mary and I had eaten late. Well, I'd eaten late. Mary had just smoked. Said she was too wound up. I heated up the crumbed fish fillets with potato wedges from the freezer and some frozen peas. I made a plate for Dad and put it in the microwave.

Sometimes he wanted food when he came home late. Sometimes he didn't, but it wasn't worth taking the chance. After I had cleared up the dishes, Mary and I worked on the costume. It was fun. A complete disaster, but fun. It cleared my head of stuff.

Now, though, lying in the dark with night noises all around, I thought about what Leah and I had decided to do. It was simple enough. In theory at least. And it would give us proof. If it worked. Of course, none of that would matter if I couldn't even get to sleep. But the more I tried, the more awake I became. I sipped water from the glass on my bedside table and checked the clock. It was 12:30 a.m. I had been thrashing around in bed for two hours. Dad would be home any minute. I was praying he wouldn't smell cigarette smoke in the kitchen. I couldn't face the satin shorts, the gloves, the strange dance under harsh fluorescent lights.

I heard a key in the lock, followed by the grating of the front door. It was slightly warped, probably with the humidity, and wasn't a good fit in the frame. I listened to the clatter of car keys on the kitchen table and the fridge door opening and closing. A click as the overhead fan was switched on and then the back door opened. Silence. I turned my back to the door and tried to settle again. At least Dad didn't seem to be the worse for grog. I could tell from the sounds.

I was aware of changes to my body, the relaxation of muscles, the slow thudding of my heart as I rode toward sleep. And then the door swung open, and a wedge of light flooded the bed. I pulled the sheet over my nakedness and rolled toward the door. Maybe I should have pretended I was asleep. But that had never made any difference in the past.

Dad stood for a while, looking at me. He didn't seem drunk, though I noticed a slight swaying. The expression on his face was not angry, but I couldn't really read it. After all this time, I still couldn't read his moods accurately. Not one hundred percent. My mouth felt dry and my tongue thick. I sat up and gulped more water. Dad stood a few moments longer and then sat on the bed next to me. The silence was heavy. I couldn't help myself. I had to break it.

"How was work, Dad?" I said.

He rubbed his hands over the stubble of his chin.

"Ah, you know, Michael," he said. "Work is work. Has to be done. What about you? How was school?"

"Okay."

"I got a phone call today. About a meeting at your school tomorrow?"

"I know. Sorry."

"So what's going on?"

His voice wasn't angry, and I relaxed a little. Maybe the gloves wouldn't come out tonight.

"They wouldn't tell me much over the phone, just that it was about your progress so far, a new school, a few issues. Blah, blah, blah."

I shrugged.

"Are you getting bullied again?"

I weighed up the options. I could lie, but Dad probably wouldn't believe me. Anyway, there was no point, what with the meeting tomorrow. But then the truth always had a price tag. I was too tired to talk about cowardice, the wisdom of fighting back, that it was all in the eyes, that the power came from the shoulder, that the key was movement. Keep moving, son. Sometimes, though, you don't have any choices.

"A bit. It'll settle down."

Dad sighed and laced his fingers over his knee. I had expected anger, but he just seemed tired and calm. In a strange way, that worried me more than anger. I knew what to expect from anger.

There was another stretch of silence. I took a sip of milk and glanced around the room for differences. I didn't think I'd fallen asleep, but sometimes it's difficult to tell. Nothing.

"What are we going to do, Michael?" he said. His voice was small, defeated.

I rubbed a thin trickle of sweat from the side of my face. "About what?" I said.

"Everything," he replied. "What are we going to do about everything?"

I didn't say anything. I didn't understand the question. A number on my alarm clock flickered and changed. I sat up farther in bed and pulled the sheet around my legs.

"I'm thinking of moving on, Michael. What do ya reckon?"

My heart thumped. I nearly blurted out that our bags weren't even unpacked, that we'd just got here, that I'd finished only three days at school. But I didn't. I shrugged. Dad rubbed at the bridge of his nose.

"I don't like it here, Michael. In fact, I hate it. It's a shitty place."

He'd said that about the last place. And the place before that. I felt panic at the thought of another frantic round of packing, loading the truck, and taking off down dusty roads for hundreds of kilometers, picking a place on the map at random. Finding a house no one else wanted to live in because it was in desperate need of renovation, or there was evidence of a recent rat infestation, or the electrics were dodgy. Starting yet another school, watching out for the kids with cold eyes. And for what? So that in a month or two, or half a year, Dad would say we were going again, that the place was driving him mad. I suddenly realized I didn't want to leave this town. I didn't want to leave Millways. I didn't want to leave Leah. I was tired of running, chasing Dad's dreams. Or escaping his nightmares. Yet I didn't tell him that. I didn't have the courage. Coward, see? Somone told me once that some victims enjoy being victims, encourage it even. That was me. I let everyone bully me because deep down I liked it. I nearly cried at the thought.

"Do you miss your mum, Michael?" asked Dad.

It was like a jolt of electricity passed through me. Dad hardly ever mentioned Mum. I didn't know why he was doing it now.

"I miss her," he continued. "Sometimes I think I miss her more now than I did just after she died. You know, they tell you things will get better, Michael, that time will heal. But it's a lie. It doesn't get better. It will never get better."

I bit at my fingernails. I saw, with something approaching horror, that Dad was crying. His face was twisted with the effort of keeping it in, but a tear was crawling down his cheek. I felt embarrassed, as though I had caught him naked. At that moment I would have been happier out in the backyard, the gloves on, circling. It was so strange. I wanted to reach out, touch him, but we didn't do that. The past weighed my hand down. Dad gulped and wiped his cheek as if angry at his own weakness.

"I miss her too, Dad," I said finally.

It was the closest I could come to touching him. I wanted to say that I felt angry as well. Angry at her for leaving us. That if I could bring her back from the dead, it would be to yell at her, punish her for what she'd done to us. How dare she? And I wanted to tell him that anger can only get you so far. Eventually, you have to stop running.

Dad nodded. His body shuddered slightly, as if he was mentally pulling himself together. His shoulders straightened.

"I know you do, son," he said. "I know you do." He tried to smile at me, but it came out wrong—weak and helpless. "And maybe I'll think about the moving thing a bit longer. Sometimes I get so tired of it all. I just . . . I don't know. I just want a place where I can be . . . at peace. Do you know what I mean? A place where I fit. I haven't found it yet. Maybe it's time to stop searching."

He stood and moved toward the door. His walk was painful, almost a shuffle. A long way from the balance on the toes, the skipping and dancing.

"Dad?" I said. He turned.

"I know it's difficult to hit a moving target, Dad. It's in the legs and in the eyes. But sometimes it's easier to just take the punch and get on with it."

He stood for a long moment, then laughed. He straightened and laughed and angled his head to one side.

"And when did you get so smart, eh, Michael?" he said. "Who gave you permission to grow up?"

I shrugged. He took a step back into the room.

"You know, it's the strangest thing," he said. "I came in here to yell at you. Right up to the moment I saw you lying in bed I was going to give you heaps. It stinks of cigarettes in the kitchen. You can't even be bothered to smoke outside, where I can't smell it. And there's money missing from the pot. You tried to cover it up, but you can't fool me. Spent on cigarettes, of course."

I opened my mouth, but he raised his hand.

"Let me finish," he continued. "It's important. When I saw

you lying there, I saw your mother. Something in your mouth, the expression in your eyes. And I thought that if you're smoking—and stealing money to do it—well, that's partly my fault, isn't it? I've been a crap father, Michael. I haven't paid enough attention. You're overweight because you're unhappy. Smoking and pinching money. Maybe I should stop shifting the blame. That's all I wanted to say. Get some sleep now. Good night, son."

"Good night, Dad."

He had almost closed the door before he stuck his head back in.

"But cut out the smoking, okay? It stunts your growth. So will stealing, if I catch you at it again."

The light from the corridor snapped off as the door closed and the darkness pressed upon me. Too many things to think about. I didn't know if I would ever get to sleep. I turned on my light. Reading helped sometimes. So I got the book out of my bedside drawer. The print was small and that would probably help. Tire me out. Within fifteen minutes I wouldn't be able to keep my eyes open. Maybe.

One of the things Dad had tried after Mum died was religion. He'd been right into it for a month or so. Then he wasn't. Maybe it was because it didn't pack the immediate punch of alcohol. I don't know. But for that month we'd gone to church, I went to Sunday school. And I liked it. No one bullied me there, for one thing. Then one day we simply didn't go. I'd got dressed in my good clothes and everything, but Dad was facedown on the kitchen table, bottles all around. I missed going to church. It had felt safe there. But I still had the Bible they'd given me. I dipped into it occasionally. It gave me comfort, though I never talked to anyone about it. It was something I wanted to keep to myself. Sometimes I felt it was telling me stuff, for my ears only.

Thursday

1.

My chest heaved. I sat upright in bed and stared, unseeing, into the darkness. Blood was thunder in my ears, sweat clammy on my face. I took deep, gulping breaths. So close this time. One hand brushing the glass before the explosion of color brought me back to this, the grainy blackness and the pulse of sound.

It took a few moments before I realized the pulse was outside the room. As my heartbeat slowed, I was able to focus on the sound. A double blurt. Rhythmical. I swung my legs out of bed and glanced at the green digits of the clock. Six-thirty. Who'd be ringing at this time? I felt around and grabbed the first thing I could find on the floor. The silk of the boxing shorts was smooth against my skin. I stumbled getting into them. By the time I got to the phone, I thought the whole neighborhood would have woken.

"Hello?"

"I'm outside, Michael."

"Leah?" I cupped my hand over the receiver. "What are you talking about? Do you know what time it is?"

"Come outside. Now. I've got something to show you." She hung up.

I was still dizzy from sleep. I should have realized what this meant, but I didn't. I crept back to my bedroom, found another pair of shorts and a dark T-shirt. When I pulled the curtains back, dawn was a bloodstain on the sky. I tried to spot Leah, but there were too many shadows. I eased my bedroom door shut. One hinge had a habit of squeaking. I went down the corridor to the kitchen door. It was quieter than the front door, though it still grated when I pulled it open. I stopped and listened. Nothing except the sound of my own breathing.

Leah was behind a palm tree. She looked at me, serious.

"Leah, what the . . ."

She ducked down behind the tree. When she appeared again, she had Scamp in her arms. He wriggled. She put her mouth close to his ear.

"Do you want to see Michael, Scamp? Do you?"

And he could. I took him from Leah's arms, and he looked

up at me, and his eyes were bright and clear and shining. He licked my hand. I felt something tightening in my chest. There were tears in Leah's eyes.

"Do you know what this means, Michael?" she whispered. "Have you any idea?"

I held up my hand. There was a sound of a toilet flushing in the house. I could see a dim light in the bathroom.

"You'd better go, Leah," I said. "I have to go in. I'll talk to you at school."

I didn't wait for a reply. As I bundled Scamp into her arms, I was already moving back toward the kitchen.

I'd found Scamp curled at the foot of Leah's bed. I hadn't woken her. I'd wanted to concentrate on one thing only. Scamp had woken, though. He'd jumped up on his stubby legs, tail windmilling. I'd sat on the edge of the bed, and he'd leapt into my lap, twisting onto his back. I'd rubbed his hairless belly, my nerves tingling. Before, this had all been a game. Now there was something—everything—at stake. I'd turned him over, and he'd looked up at me, his eyes cloudy. I'd put my hands on his head.

I'd been able to sense the milky film of blindness, and the clear, healthy jelly beneath. I'd placed one hand over his eyes. Scamp had kept still, as if he'd known what I was doing. I'd gathered the thin film into my hand and drawn it like ink into blotting paper. It was easy. When I'd taken my hand away, there were two distorted reflections of the window in his eyes. I'd known they would be deep brown, almost black. Scamp had shaken his head. I'd watched his pupils dilate.

I sat at the kitchen table and put my head into my hands. Images spun and thoughts jumbled. I didn't even hear the kitchen door when it opened. I jumped when Mary put her hand on my shoulder.

"Are you all right, Michael?" she said. "You look like you've seen a ghost."

I pinched myself hard on the fleshy part of my forearm. In the early days, that would wake me if I was in the Dream, though for the last year or so I could do that and still stay asleep. So I checked for differences as well. I didn't want to suddenly find myself in bed. I needed this to be real.

"I'm fine, Mary," I said. "Just tired, I guess. I had a restless night."

"Did I hear the phone?"

"Wrong number."

Mary took a pack of cigarettes and a lighter from her bag. I hardly noticed. But my words were automatic.

"You'd better smoke outside. Dad'll go nuts."

"Okay, sweetie. Get some breakfast. Are you sure you're well enough for school? You can always ring in sick, you know."

"I'm fine," I said. "I wouldn't miss school for the world."

• • •

Nobody bothered me on the bus. I had calmed down a little, but I still needed space to think. It would take time before it all sank in. Kids got on. I heard the chatter all around—films that had been watched, students who would get bashed if they weren't careful, homework that wasn't done or done badly. Noise washed over me, but it was from a world I'd outgrown. It wouldn't have bothered me if Martin Leechy had got on. There was no reason to be scared of him anymore. But he didn't get on. Neither did Leah. I sat alone at the front of the bus. Kids stood all along the aisle. No one wanted to take the empty space next to me. It didn't matter.

I looked for Leah in the school yard. She would want to talk. But she was nowhere to be seen. The sun was building strength. Even at eight in the morning it was hot. I stood alone in the center of the yard. The shaded areas were thick with kids. My face prickled with sweat, but I shivered.

The bell rang and I joined the swarm toward Home Groups. I reached the first floor, and Martin Leechy fell in beside me. I carried on walking, but he grabbed my arm.

"What's your hurry, Michael?" he said.

I stopped and faced him. I waited until the other kids had disappeared. We were alone in the corridor. I looked into his brown eyes. I'd never seen fear in them. I'd never seen anything in them except ice. But I would. I made myself a promise.

"Never in too much of a hurry for you, Martin," I replied, smiling. "How can I be of assistance?"

There was the faintest flash of irritation, and then his eyes were blank again. Even so, I felt a cold joy that I had touched him. The muscles of his mouth tensed for a moment and then relaxed into a smile.

"Feeling good today, are we, Michael? Excellent. I'm glad to hear it. I don't suppose there's any chance of a chat at recess, is there? I mean, I know a popular guy like you won't have too many gaps in his social calendar, but I would be grateful for a word."

I patted him on the shoulder.

"Consider it done, Martin," I said. "Recess. On the oval. Looking forward to it. Now, if you'll excuse me, I have to get to Home Group. Catch you later."

I walked off and it felt good. I didn't turn around. I didn't feel the need.

I opened the door of A15 and walked in. The sun slanted through the windows, and I felt the warmth, the coziness of the room. Happiness should exist here. Students sat in small groups, but Leah was not among them. Mr. Atkins was behind his desk, marking the roll. His glasses had slipped down his nose, and he was peering over them, his brow rumpled. I walked up to him.

"Ah, Michael," he said. "Good to see you, young man."

"And you, sir."

"Draw up a pew, Mr. Terny. Home Group is the ideal time

to make contact, touch minds, chew the proverbial fat. Park yourself, young man, and let's communicate."

I pulled up a chair. I wanted to see what was in Mr. Atkins's eyes. I expected joy, peace, calmness. But instead there was worry. Worry and a touch of fear. That was strange. That wasn't right. I made up my mind to find out why.

Mr. Atkins examined me for a while. He took off his glasses and chewed the ends.

"Is that a bruise on your cheek, Michael? It seems a bit red."

I touched my cheek. It felt slightly tender. That was interesting. Something else to think about.

"Walked into a door, sir," I said.

"Ah, a door," he said. "You don't make a habit of that, by any chance?"

"No, sir."

"I'm relieved to hear it." He paused. "I heard about math class yesterday, Michael. Do you want to talk about it?" I liked the way his words changed. I knew he was concerned, of course. But I liked how he could switch from dazzling words to simple language. It made me feel I was important.

"I messed up, Mr. Atkins. It won't happen again."

He nodded but my words didn't seem to help. He glanced down at his roll. I was surprised. He didn't normally break eye contact. There was something really bothering him.

"And what about other things, Michael? Miss Palmer had

a word with me yesterday. Are you feeling fine? Anything on your mind?"

"Plenty on my mind, sir. But it's all good. I'm feeling great. Seriously. Never better."

Mr. Atkins kept his head down. I sensed he was wrestling with something. As if he wanted to say more but couldn't find the right words. It was difficult to believe Mr. Atkins would ever have that problem. Then he lifted his head as if he had made a decision. He snapped his glasses back on, and the eyes were smiling again. At least they were smiling on the surface.

"I confess that you exude an air of the upbeat, Michael, and that is, without doubt, cause for rejoicing. Now, carpe diem has always struck me as an admirable philosophy. What is your take on that?"

"Sir?"

"Seize the day, my boy. I recollect that yesterday you said you intended to grace the Year Ten Social with your presence. I trust you haven't changed your mind?"

"No, sir."

"Excellent. Excellent. In which case, I can provide you with a ticket. A bargain basement ten dollars to you. Actually," he said, lowering his voice, "it's ten dollars for everyone, but I'm trying to raise my profile as a good guy by giving my Home Group the impression I'm offering discounts."

I handed him ten dollars and asked for a receipt. I'd taken

the money from the pot this morning. Dad didn't know, but at least the receipt would show I hadn't spent it on anything else. Then I caught myself. I almost smiled. I didn't need to worry about receipts anymore. But old habits die hard, I guess. Mr. Atkins seemed surprised, but he fumbled in his desk drawer and pulled out a battered receipt book. He scribbled on a sheet and handed it to me.

"Not a tax scam, is it, Michael?"

"Sir?"

"Never mind. Well, it's been good doing business with you. Have a splendid day, my friend."

"Sir? Haven't you forgotten something, sir?" Mr. Atkins looked blank. "The ticket, sir."

"Ah, the ticket. Well, I think you'll find it's in your pocket."

It was too. I hadn't seen a thing. He winked at me.

"Small magic, my boy."

The door to the classroom opened and Leah came in. She was flushed and breathless, as if she'd been running. She stopped when she saw me. I smiled.

You and me, I said to myself. You and me are going to rule the world.

2.

We didn't get a chance to talk until recess. We had separate classes, though I couldn't tell you what they were. I wrote down what I was supposed to write down, but my mind was elsewhere. Nobody said anything to me and that was good.

When the bell rang, I wandered over to my tree. The world was different, the sky a crisp blue I'd never seen before. Clouds were more textured, the wind fresher. My skin tingled. Happiness coursed through me like a drug. When Leah came and sat beside me, taking my hand in hers, it seemed to make the world perfect.

"How did you do it, Michael?" she said. "I woke up at about six o'clock and Scamp was there, on the pillow next to me.

Looking at me. With those big brown eyes. It was . . . I felt . . . Oh hell, I can't describe it. How did you do it?"

"I don't know," I replied. I didn't either. The twist to bring two worlds together. That's what she meant. Perhaps I didn't have to think about it at all. Just being able to ride the Dream was enough. Or maybe I did something but didn't know how I'd done it. "But I suppose it doesn't really matter, does it? I can do it. That's the important thing."

"Oh, Michael. Think about it. The possibilities. You've cured Mrs. Atkins; Scamp can see. There's no limit to the good you can do in the world. Diseases will be a thing of the past. No more pain, no suffering, no kids dying of starvation. You could end wars. Think of that."

"Do it in my sleep, Leah." I loved her intensity. Her eyes were glowing with passion. "Though it might take me time to get around the whole world. I mean, I can only put in an average eight hours a night. Let's hope I don't get insomnia." I was just kidding around, but she suddenly gripped my hand.

"But I thought you'd made it so the Dream and the real world were one thing. Like that paper strip you told me about."

"The Möbius strip was just an image, Leah. I don't know how this works. But I do know that when I'm not asleep, I'm just fat old Michael Terny. Not a superman. I can't do anything here. But who knows? Maybe one day. For the time being, I'll settle for the Dream."

For a while neither of us said anything. I could tell she was fantasizing about curing cancer patients and AIDS sufferers, about me moving unseen through hospital wards, removing, little by little, the pain from the world. I thought about that as well. But I also considered other things. I could cure pain and I could create it. I wondered how difficult it would be to track a person down. Someone from the past whose name I didn't know, whose appearance and whereabouts were a mystery. Someone who had gotten drunk nearly ten years ago and decided it was a good idea to get in a car.

"Your cheek is red. Is that a bruise?" Leah touched it gently.

I laughed. "I walked into your bedroom door. Seems like Scamp wasn't the only one to keep a reminder of what happened last night."

A shadow fell across the grass. I'd forgotten Martin Leechy and the appointment. He looked down at us, a small smile on his lips. I stared back. I had the courage now. Olive skin, high cheekbones. Teeth white and even, dark hair gelled. Expensive clothes. If I could have invented someone completely the opposite of me in every way, it would have been Martin.

"Forgot our little arrangement, huh, Michael?" he said.

"I did, actually, Martin," I replied. "Sorry about that. Mind like a sieve."

I saw the tiny flash of irritation again. I nearly smiled.

"However," I continued, "I can spare you a few minutes now, if that's convenient."

Martin glanced at Leah.

"In private?" he said.

I noticed it was a request and not a statement. I turned to Leah.

"Would you excuse us?" I said.

Leah didn't want to leave. Her face was creased with worry.

"I'll catch up in English," I continued. "Save me a seat. It's okay. Seriously. Martin and I just need to discuss a few matters."

"Don't worry, Leah," said Martin. "You'll get your boyfriend back in one piece. I only want to chat with him."

Leah stood and brushed grass from her skirt. She threw Martin a look full of hatred. I was surprised he didn't feel it like a fist. She walked across the oval toward the canteen while Martin and I watched. Only when the crowd of students swallowed her up did Martin sit down.

"She's really keen on you, mate," he said.

"I know," I said. I couldn't believe how good it was to say that, to feel it.

"You've changed," said Martin. "Something about you."

"I know," I said again. "I have changed. I've lost my fear. And what's more, I don't believe it's coming back."

Martin cracked his knuckles.

"That's good," he said. "That's progress. Fear cripples you. It stops you doing what you feel like, when you feel like it. Nearly everyone suffers from it. They call it different things—morality, conscience, ethics. Labels to make themselves feel good about their fear—but that's what it comes down to. Scared of taking what you want for no other reason than you want it. To make people suffer just because you can. You know something, Mikey? I think that's the greatest pleasure in the world."

I locked my fingers around my knees and followed the flight patterns of three kites that were circling something on the oval. Maybe it was a lizard. Suddenly one of the kites swooped down, brushing the grass. It gripped something small in its talons. Death was all around.

"Has it ever occurred to you that you're a psychopath, Martin?" I said.

He laughed.

"Many times, mate," he said. "But even psychopaths need fun. Especially psychopaths, actually. And anyway, Michael, stop kidding yourself. That's what I was talking about before. You want to feel good about yourself, so you attach labels to me. But tell me this. And be honest. Isn't there someone out there who you'd like to kill? Someone who's made you suffer, someone who hurt a person you cared about? Of course there is. And if you could get them at your mercy, you wouldn't be satisfied with justice. You'd want to taste their pain. You'd want to bathe in their suffering. And you'd enjoy it. I know you better than you know yourself. Remember that, Michael."

"I'm not scared of you anymore, Martin."

He put his arm around my shoulder. My flesh shrank from his touch, but I didn't move. I didn't want him to misinterpret it as fear. He moved his mouth close to my left ear.

"I don't want you to be scared of me, Mikey. You don't understand. Not yet. But you're getting closer. All I want is for you to stop being scared of yourself. It's that simple. And when you truly know yourself, when all the fear has gone, then I'll help you. I'm no different from Leah in that regard. We just have different things to offer."

I stood up. I was tired of this. I brushed grass from my legs.

"You talk in riddles, Martin. And I'm tired of it. I don't want to waste my time with it. You rub chocolate cake in my face and punch me, and now you try to confuse me by babbling on about not fearing myself. I know you are trying to terrify me physically and emotionally. Drive me mad. Well, I'm not playing the game anymore. Play with yourself, Martin. It's about all you're good for."

I walked across the oval toward the canteen. I didn't look back. I didn't respond when he called after me.

"I just want to help you, Michael. You'll see. Soon you'll see how much you need me. At the Social, Michael. I'll show you at the Social."

I kept on walking. The kites circled overhead.

3.

Y do u want 2 go?

Leah's handwriting was large and rounded. Almost childish. It was a lot like my own and I felt pleased. Another thing we had in common. She pushed my exercise book back across the desk. I kept one eye on the teacher, but she was reading to us from a novel and hardly looked up from the page. I wrote slowly and lightly, so the sound of the pencil wouldn't draw attention.

Mr. A. He seems sad + worried.

Wot r u thinking?

I want 2 check.

Ditching?

Y not?

I h8 ditchers.

U don't have 2 come.

Try stopping me.

It was really easy to get out of school without anyone seeing us. When the bell went, Leah and I mingled with the swarming students. No one paid attention as we slipped into the yard and out the gate. I felt guilty. It was stupid, but I'd never felt comfortable breaking rules. I supposed I'd have to get used to it. After all, in the Dream I made my own rules.

As I crossed the road, I glanced back at the school. Its concrete face and blank, staring windows didn't seem to care one way or another.

I had some difficulty finding the house. I wasn't even sure it was the right place until I saw the dog lying in the driveway. Now that it came down to it, I felt nervous again, and Leah had to open the gate and ring the doorbell. I stayed behind her, as if hiding.

This time the footsteps approaching were stronger. Feet hit the floor rather than scuffing over it. I started to hope again. Mrs. Atkins opened the door and cocked her head to one side as she looked at Leah. Her smile was polite.

"Yes?" she said. "Can I help you?"

Leah didn't answer. She simply stepped to one side. Mrs. Atkins's smile slipped. I saw a struggle in her face, doubts that left marks in her eyes. I took a step forward.

"Mrs. Atkins," I said. "My name is Michael. I think we've met before."

She looked me up and down. Then her smile returned.

"Yes. Yes, I believe we have, Michael. Please come in."

We had tea and biscuits. We talked. I hadn't planned this. Not really. But Mr. Atkins had been worrying me since Home Group. His sad eyes, the sense of pain and concern. None of that should have been there. Not if I had cured Mrs. Atkins, like I'd cured Scamp. I had to know. One way or another I had to know. When I'd explained this to Leah on our walk, she'd seen the sense of it straightaway. But it wasn't as simple as that. It was only when we'd left the school that I'd had the time to think about it properly. How could I ask someone, a total stranger, if their cancer had miraculously disappeared? A cancer I shouldn't have any idea existed in the first place. What could I say? "I think I came to you in a dream, Mrs. Atkins, and took away your tumor. I can do stuff like that. Feel like giving me an update?"

When I'd told Leah of my concerns, she'd snorted.

"Worried about making a fool of yourself, Michael? Think that's important? Let's just go. See what happens."

As it turned out, I didn't even have to bring the subject up. Mrs. Atkins did. We sat in the same room as before. Everything was identical, apart from Leah sitting opposite me, a cup of tea in one hand and a plate of biscuits balanced on her knee. The bowl of sugar cubes was on the table between us. Mrs. Atkins talked about the weather and how nice it was to have visitors. I looked for signs in her face and the way she sat in her chair. Signs of wholeness, the absence of darkness behind the skull. But it's all different when you're not in the Dream. I wasn't sure. I didn't say much. Finally, Mrs. Atkins put her cup down on the table and clasped her hands in her lap. I knew what was coming was important.

"I have to thank you, Michael. Putting it into words would sound ridiculous. But I think you have come here today in search of an answer. Well, I believe the answer is yes. I believe. I won't know for sure until I go to see my consultant. Get some tests. But I feel . . . I feel, strongly, that what was wrong with me is no longer wrong. And that you had something to do with it. Everything to do with it. Does that make sense?"

I nodded. Suddenly I had an urge to get out of there. I put my half-empty cup down on the table and stood.

"We'd better go, Mrs. Atkins," I said.

"Wait a moment, Michael," said Leah. "I want to know more." She turned to Mrs. Atkins. "How do you know this?"

I sat down again.

Mrs. Atkins was silent for a long while. I wasn't even sure she was going to answer. But then she gave a slight smile.

"I'm so sorry," she said. "I was thinking about my husband.

He . . . He's a magician, you know. Tricks. Coins out of ears, rabbits out of hats. He loves it. He loves the idea of the impossible. It's what he said drew him into teaching. But he's also got another side. Rational. Everything can be explained. He knows I'm going to die. He's known for months. It makes sense to him. Even though it's also destroying him." She laughed. "And now I can't say anything. Not until I go through the whole thing with scans and doctors' reports. Until I have something on a medical report that says it scientifically. A miracle. Except they'll call it *remission*. But it's the same thing. It just sounds more respectable." Mrs. Atkins picked up her cup again. "Isn't that strange? I can't tell him what I know. You see, my dear, I'd have to tell him what I'm telling you now. That, in a dream, a boy touched my head and took away the cancer that was killing me. But I can't tell him. Not yet." Her voice broke and I thought she was going to cry.

"We'd better go, Mrs. Atkins," I said. This time Leah got up with me. We went to the front door. Mrs. Atkins shook our hands. She held on to mine for longer than she needed to. I didn't know what to say.

"I'm really pleased, Mrs. Atkins," I said eventually. "And we won't say a word to your husband."

"You are destined for greatness," she said. Her voice was low and intense. "To bring happiness into the world, by driving out the darkness." She nodded at Leah. "She knows it. I know it. You're the miracle, Michael. You."

We left then. I glanced back once and Mrs. Atkins was still at the door. She gave a half-wave. Leah and I walked back to school, and we didn't say a word. I looked at the sky and the trees and the birds. The world was full of possibilities.

When we got back, the school yard was busy with students. Leah and I waited until the teacher on lunch duty had gone around a corner, and then we slipped in through the gates. Leah went off to get some food from the canteen while there was still something left. I wasn't hungry. For once. And I didn't feel like going back to my tree.

So I stood in the yard, my mind swirling. The sun was fierce. I could feel it burning the top of my head, but it didn't seem to matter. I stood surrounded by a shimmering sea of asphalt. Kites circled overhead.

When Miss Palmer touched me on the arm, I didn't react. She had to stand in front of me. Maybe I was almost asleep. Standing asleep. It would be useful if I could do that.

"Michael, are you all right?" said Miss Palmer. Her voice was strange and distant. I almost had to snap myself back into my body.

"Fine, miss. Thanks," I added.

"Aren't you hot, Michael?"

I was. Now that she mentioned it, I was very hot. I felt dizzy.

"You'll dehydrate," she said. "Come on. Come with me."

She led me to the bubblers. I noticed, in a vague sort of way, that when I got there, all the other kids left. Miss Palmer made me drink. Not just a couple of mouthfuls, but huge gulps. The water felt good where it splashed on my face. Miss Palmer offered me a clean handkerchief, which I wet and pressed on the back of my neck. When I straightened up, I could see she was worried about me. The eyes don't lie.

"What were you doing, Michael? Standing in the full sun. You know better than that, don't you? Look at me, Michael."

I did. Her eyes softened.

"I saw you from the staff room. It's dangerous, Michael."

"I'm fine, miss. Thank you."

The bell went. I had math next. Miss Palmer wanted me to go to the nurse, but I refused. She made me drink some more water, though. I wasn't allowed to go to class until I had. It sloshed around in my stomach and made me uncomfortable. As she walked off, she still looked doubtful. I watched her go.

"I'm destined for greatness," I said. But I said it quietly and she didn't hear. Even so, she glanced back at me. When I had time, one night, I'd do something about that worry in her eyes. It couldn't be healthy.

I joined my class outside the math room. The door was locked and students were milling around. There was no sign of Mr. Williams. A few boys were jostling each other, hot, sweaty, and pumped with energy after playing football on the oval. I didn't know their names. Except Jamie Archer. He hadn't seen me, so I sat on the floor, back against the wall. He didn't worry me. I just wasn't in the mood. Jamie had another kid in a headlock and was rubbing his knuckles into the boy's scalp. They were both laughing. Finally, Jamie pushed him away.

"You're fuckin' gay, Kyle."

The other boy rubbed snot from his nose with a sleeve.

"Oh yeah?" he said, laughing. "Well, it wasn't me grabbin' someone by the head and runnin' my hands over him, was it, Jamie? Ya poof."

"You're so fuckin' gay you should be in Atkins's Home Group."

Some of the other boys, who were leaning against the wall and watching, howled with laughter. A couple of the girls joined in, but most kept their distance.

"Yeah, Kyle. I reckon he fancies you."

"Fuck off!"

"Give us a kiss, Kyle."

"You'd be great together. A double act. Ben Down and Phil Macafferty."

The screams of laughter intensified. Kyle had bad acne and a stupid face. He cast around for support but couldn't find any. His dull, heavy features fell. He was trapped. I could see it in his eyes. He wanted a way out.

"You wouldn't catch me in the same room as that arse bandit," he said finally. I knew what he wanted. It wasn't a way out, after all. It was a way back in. He hoped his words might buy him a ticket. "That poof. He makes me puke. They shouldn't have him here, among kids. Friggin' pedophile."

"Mr. Atkins isn't gay," I said. "And, anyway, pedophiles are rarely homosexual."

I hadn't spoken loudly, but my words fell into a brief noiseless space. Kyle turned toward me, his sleeve rubbing again at his nose. Everyone stared at me. Jamie Archer pushed through a knot of boys.

"What did you say?"

"Mr. Atkins isn't gay. He has a wife."

Archer moved a step closer, his lips twisted. I could see his yellow teeth.

"And what do you know about it, ya fat bastard? You've only been here five fuckin' minutes, Wrenbury. Suddenly you're an expert?"

I stood up.

"He isn't gay," I repeated. My voice did not shake. And that was another miracle. I looked directly into Jamie Archer's eyes and felt good. We stared at each other for about ten seconds. Then he punched me in the face. I didn't even see it coming. One moment I was standing my ground, the next I was on my back on the hard floor and a trickle of blood was running from my nose. Numbness spread across my face. Archer aimed a kick at my head, but I grabbed his ankle and twisted so he fell on top of me. He grabbed me by the front of my T-shirt and drew his fist back to hit me again, but I managed to roll over, pinning him. I pushed down with all my weight on his chest so he couldn't move. Our faces were millimeters apart. A few drops of sweat-soaked blood dripped from the end of my nose onto him.

"Listen, you bastard," I whispered. "Because I'm telling you something, Archer, and you need to listen. You've just been promoted to number one on my list. I'll be coming for you, Archer. Tonight. When you're asleep. When you think you are safe. I'll be there. And I'll rip your heart out and feed it to you. Do you understand, Archer? Do you?"

Maybe it was in my eyes. They felt hard with hatred. Perhaps it was my voice, quiet and serious. Archer suddenly seemed like a little kid, terrified of the dark. His bottom lip quivered, and his eyes swam with moisture. In their wetness I could see my own reflection, distorted. Archer didn't get a chance to say anything. Suddenly I was dragged to my feet and pinned to the wall.

Mr. Williams had arrived for his math class.

4.

Miss Palmer's office was prickling with tension. I was in the chair by the door, Jamie in the corner, Miss Palmer in the middle. Keeping us at a distance.

Mr. Williams took us both down there. Immediately. He didn't even ask for an explanation. The help line poster was still on the wall, but it didn't command my interest anymore. I kept my eyes on Miss Palmer.

"What happened, Michael?"

I gave it some thought. I wanted to choose my words carefully. I wanted Miss Palmer to see me as a responsible, composed person. When I took the wad away from my nose, the bleeding had nearly stopped. I folded the tissue neatly and crossed my legs.

"A disagreement, miss."

"Jamie?"

"He's off his fuckin' head, Miss—"

"Jamie!"

It was clear who was the mature student in this situation. Miss Palmer could see that. Anyone could see that. I kept a dignified silence as Jamie carried on.

"Sorry, miss, but he is. He threatened to kill me, and he mutters all the time. He's a weirdo. He don't belong here. . . ."

I watched Jamie calmly. I examined him as if he were a bug I could crush beneath my heel. His face was red and blotchy from crying. He tried to hide it, but tears spread over his acne and dripped from his chin. A real mess. Scared. Of me. I tried to find pity for him, but it wasn't there. I had known boys like Jamie for years. He fed on fear, provided it was other people's. I had no pity for him and those like him. Only justice.

He blubbered on, but I didn't pay attention. Finally, Miss Palmer turned to me.

"Is this true, Michael? Did you threaten to kill him?"

I considered my words.

"I think what I actually said was that I would rip his heart out and feed it to him. I suppose you could interpret that as a death threat."

Miss Palmer tried to keep her expression neutral. But she couldn't hide from me. I caught a glimpse of fear in her eyes, quickly replaced by another emotion. A grudging admiration for my calmness of manner and the precise way in which I was answering her questions. I continued, my voice steady and measured.

"As you can tell from the words I used, I was emotional. But it's also obvious that such a threat is foolish." I opened my arms wide. "I mean, look at me. Is it likely I could follow through with a threat like that?"

Archer rubbed at his eyes and leaned forward anxiously. "You didn't see him, miss."

Miss Palmer held up a hand for silence. She didn't take her eyes off me.

"And what was it, precisely, that made you so emotional, Michael? What triggered this threat?"

"He called Mr. Atkins gay."

"I never—"

"Quiet, please, Jamie," said Miss Palmer. "I want to hear what Michael has to say. Michael, why would you get so angry about such a comment?"

I thought again. I folded my hands under my chin.

"Because it's unjust, miss. Injustice angers me."

Miss Palmer leaned back in her chair, and I dabbed at my nose with a clean tissue. The flow had stopped. There was silence for a while and then she stood.

"Right," she said. "I want both of you to put your sides of the story in writing. But first, I think the nurse should check you out. Jamie, you come with me. Michael, there is a notepad and a pen on my desk. Start writing. Write everything down, just as it happened."

Miss Palmer opened the door and waved for Jamie to follow her. At the last moment, Jamie leaned down and whispered, though he didn't stop moving, "You're fuckin' dead, Terny."

It was peaceful in the room after they left. Just the faint ticking of the clock on the wall. I reached for the notepad. I didn't start writing immediately, though. I thought it all over. I wanted my evidence to be logical and clearly written. It wouldn't matter, of course. Not in the long run. But I knew that when I started to make things happen, as Dreamrider, it would be good if people knew me as someone who was clear-thinking. Not just a kid with more power than he could handle. Besides, I wanted Miss Palmer to think well of me. I liked her.

And I think she was beginning to admire me.

5.

Dad was in a bad mood. He'd had to take time off work, and it had annoyed him. I could see it in his eyes. And the way he wore his filthy black undershirt and stained gray shorts. The stubble on his chin. He wanted to draw attention to the difference between them. Miss Palmer in her smart dress, Mr. Atkins in neat slacks and short-sleeved shirt. Dad was the worker. He wanted to make them feel small.

"So what are you saying? Exactly."

I sat next to him in Miss Palmer's office. I had been there the entire afternoon. Mr. Atkins sat opposite, next to Miss Palmer. Just the four of us.

"Michael is having problems, Mr. Terny," said Miss Palmer.

"Serious problems. What I'd like to do this afternoon is discuss these issues, see if we can find some common ground to address them. In particular, we'd like as much information as possible regarding Michael's previous schools and his experiences there."

Dad just looked at her. I wondered if she could see the contempt in his eyes. I hoped not.

"Jeez. You guys don't change, do you?" he said. "I ask what you're saying, exactly, and I get 'issues,' 'common ground,' and 'experiences.' You might have time to sit around here all day, but I don't. I'm losing money. So answer a simple question. Yes or no. Is Michael being bullied?"

There was a pause.

"Yes. Michael denies it, but he *is* being bullied," said Miss Palmer. I could tell she didn't want to talk about this. She had something else on her mind. I could have told her, though, that it's difficult to deflect Dad.

"And what's the school doing about it?" demanded Dad.

"All we can, Mr. Terny."

"Really?" said Dad. He was winding himself up. " 'All we can,' eh? Well, I tell ya, from where I'm sitting, that's fuck-all. I'll bet you've got the glossy brochures, though. Zero tolerance. It's horseshit. Every school's the same. 'We won't tolerate it, Mr. Terny.' 'Your son is safe with us, Mr. Terny.' But he's getting the crap bashed out of him while you lot drink tea in the staff room."

Miss Palmer leaned forward. Annoyance flared in her eyes, but when she spoke, her voice was strong.

"Mr. Terny. We have staff on yard duty at all times. We take our duty of care very seriously at Millways."

Dad snorted. "And I wouldn't mind a dollar for every time I've heard that 'duty of care' stuff either. So what's happened, huh? The ones who bullied my son. Suspended? Expelled?"

"Michael has refused to tell us who is bullying him, Mr. Terny. And we can't punish anyone unless we have evidence. You must understand that."

Dad laughed, but it was an ugly sound.

"Course he won't tell you. Whaddya expect? God, you know how this works. Rat someone out and you're dead. And that's right too. I haven't brought my son up to be a snitch. I taught him to sort things out for himself. No one respects a squealer."

"I do," said Miss Palmer. "I respect anyone who is prepared to stand up against cowards by giving the authorities the means to deal with them."

"Not in this life," said Dad. "Not my son."

"So what do you expect us to do, then, Mr. Terny? Punish everyone just on the off chance?"

Dad leaned forward. He pointed a dirty finger at Miss Palmer.

"Don't get smart," he said. "Just do your job. Is that too much to ask?"

Mr. Atkins suddenly spoke. I'd almost forgotten he was there. I think I even jumped a little.

"Mr. Terny. It's not just about bullying. We are concerned for

Michael in other ways, and we would appreciate your assistance in getting to the bottom of his troubles."

Dad leaned back and considered Mr. Atkins. He didn't give the impression of being much impressed with what he saw.

"Oh yeah? So what's the problem?"

Mr. Atkins glanced at Miss Palmer.

"I think it might be better if we had this part of the conversation in private. Michael, would you mind waiting outside for a few minutes?"

Dad shook his head and clamped his hand onto my arm. "No way," he said. "You got something to say, you say it in front of Michael."

"We really don't think that would be wise."

"It doesn't much matter what you think, does it? Michael goes, I go. Then you can talk among yourselves. Maybe that'd be better."

Miss Palmer and Mr. Atkins exchanged glances again. This wasn't going the way they wanted. Still, they seemed to reach a silent agreement. Mr. Atkins did the talking.

"Michael is behaving in ways that are causing grave concern. He is remote from other students. He retreats into worlds of his own. He talks to himself. At lunchtime he was found standing by himself in the full sun, dehydrated. We rang his previous school in Queensland. What they reported gives us even more cause for concern. They said—"

Dad got to his feet.

"C'mon, son," he said. "We're outta here."

Mr. Atkins rose as well.

"Mr. Terny, you don't understand—"

Dad raised his voice then.

"No. *You* don't understand. He's a loner. What the hell do you expect? He's bullied, he's picked on, he doesn't have friends. Jesus Christ. You are too much. And now *he's* got a problem? Let me give you some advice. Stop the bullying. That's the 'issue' here. Not what some crazed old bag in Far North Queensland says. I'm warning you. Do your job properly when he comes in tomorrow or I am going to make a whole heap of shit about this school. Do you follow me?"

"Michael will not be coming to school tomorrow." Miss Palmer's voice was firm.

Dad eyed her suspiciously. "Why not?"

"Michael was involved in a fight this afternoon, Mr. Terny," said Mr. Atkins.

Dad turned toward him.

"I saw the swollen nose," he said. "Figured he must have taken a smack. Don't tell me—no one saw who did it."

"No," said Mr. Atkins. "That's not true. One of our staff did see what happened. He saw your son with another student. Mr. Williams said Michael was behaving very violently, and he intervened because he feared for the other student's safety."

I think it was the first time Dad had looked at me since he'd entered the room. He whistled.

"You're kiddin'," he said.

"I'm afraid not. Michael has since admitted that he threatened to kill this boy. And he has shown no remorse."

Dad whistled again and then smiled broadly.

"Well, that just about beats everything," he said. "Good on you, son. Bloody oath. Good on you."

"Mr. Terny, this is a serious matter," said Miss Palmer. "We cannot allow threatening behavior in this school, regardless of provocation."

"No. You listen to me," said Dad. He pointed his finger straight at her face. "Because you don't know Michael. I do. This shit's gone on for years. Every school the same. Black eyes, cut lips. And he never stood up for himself. I told him there's only one language these bastards understand. And now you want me to be sorry he's fought back? Well, I'm not. I'm proud of him."

"The school is not proud of his actions, Mr. Terny," said Miss Palmer. "The school will not tolerate such behavior. Michael is suspended for five days. He will return only after a further interview with me, in the presence of yourself and the school counselor."

For a moment I thought Dad was going to lose it big-time. In the end, he decided on contempt.

"Come on, son," he said. "Let's get the fuck out of here."

"Michael," said Mr. Atkins. He looked at me kindly and his voice was soft. "Before you go. Is there anything you want to say?"

"Can I still come to the Social?" I said. "I mean, I know I'm suspended. But you also said I'm remote from other students and . . . Well, I'd like to go. If that's all right."

Miss Palmer and Mr. Atkins exchanged another glance. I thought I'd been pretty clever. There wasn't really anywhere for them to go. Their eyes held a conversation, a question asked and a reply received.

"Is it important to you, Michael?" asked Miss Palmer.

"Yes," I said.

I knew she understood.

"On one condition," she said finally. "That when you return to school, you cooperate fully with the school counselor. Do you promise to do that, Michael?"

"Of course," I said.

By that time, none of this would matter at all.

6.

Leah was waiting in the foyer. Dad looked straight through her. She trailed a few steps behind as Dad and I went to his truck in the front car park. He was in a good mood. The best in a very long time.

"Good on you, son," he said for the twentieth time as he opened the door of the truck. "You mark my words, those bastards won't be coming after you again in a hurry. You'll see. The hardest part is standing up to them. It'll be a lot easier from here on in."

He said other things, but I wasn't paying much attention. There was a storm blowing in from the east. The sky was darkening by the second. Clouds boiled overhead. There was a pink tinge to the air, the sun's struggle to pierce the gathering gloom. It was beautiful. I stood with my face turned to the sky, watching.

"It's that session we had last night. Reckon that was it. Power from the shoulder, eh? Keep moving, did you?"

I smiled but I didn't say anything. Dad reached into his pocket and took out his wallet. He pulled out a twenty-dollar bill.

"I can't give you a lift home, son. Every minute here is money lost. Not like those bums in there." He pointed back toward the school. "But get yourself takeout, all right? Reckon ya deserve it."

I took the money and he drove off. I watched the smoke from the truck's exhaust as it drifted and died, then tilted my head back and drank in the sky. Leah put her hand on my shoulder.

"Can I come home with you?" she asked. "You can tell me what happened in there."

I nodded. We could stop off to eat somewhere on the way home. A place that sold good fish.

"Tell me something, Leah," I said. "The clouds. The storm."

She stood next to me, and we watched the sky together. There was something about the way the clouds were boiling, the sense of huge energy building. It was like a window into myself.

"Am I making that, or is it real?" I said.

She gripped my arm.

"Do you know, Michael? I'm not sure anymore."

"Neither am I," I said. "Neither am I."

Mary didn't stop talking for half an hour. She went into instant panic as soon as she saw Leah on the doorstep. I told her we'd eaten on the way home, but she didn't listen. She bustled around the kitchen, getting crackers and dips, potato chips, and a jug of iced tea. And talked all the while. Finally, exhausted perhaps, she went into the back garden for a cigarette.

Leah and I sat at the table, picking at the crackers and dips and not saying much. I didn't feel like talking. I felt on the edge of something. I could feel it inside me. I watched Leah, her head angled down toward the table, nibbling at a biscuit. There was beauty in the sweep of her hair, the curve of her nose, a small mole, close to her right eye, that I hadn't noticed before. All of it filled me with wonder.

She held my gaze for a few moments and then smiled.

"Where are you going tonight, Michael?" she said.

The kitchen suddenly flared with lightning. Shadows fled from Leah's face. For an instant her skin was bathed in a pure light. Then darkness crashed down as thunder shook the house. Immediately there was rain, a regular drumming on the roof that built to a frenzy. All other noise was drowned. Through the kitchen window, through a haze of water, I saw Mary walk between dripping palm trees, a lit cigarette between her lips. She strolled back to the door and leaned up against its frame. I watched the end of the cigarette glow as she took another drag.

"I'll take you with me, if you like," I said.

"Should we go to the hospital? You could do good work there."

"Sure. But I have some business to attend to first."

The lightning flashed again. It made me feel strong.

"How are you, Michael?"

"Good. Yourself?"

"Can't complain, mate. Can't complain."

I switched the phone to my other ear.

"Heard you had some trouble at school today," Martin continued. "That Archer kid. No style, that guy. No style at all."

"There was no trouble."

"I heard you went mental, Michael. Feel like telling me about it?"

"No."

Martin chuckled.

"Pity. You see, the way the story goes, you nearly killed the stupid bastard. Had him on the floor. Would have beaten the shit out of him if old Williams hadn't stopped you. I wish I'd been there, Michael. Must have been a sight to behold."

I didn't say anything.

"The worm's turned, has it, Michael? That's interesting. Can I tell you a secret? You remember that thing with the cake? You think I did that just because I'm a bastard. But it's more than that. I wanted to stir you up, Michael. Get you mad. To the point where you'd fight back. After today, it looks like you should be thanking me. Whaddya reckon?"

I didn't say anything.

"So, how did it feel, Michael? When you had Archer on the floor, seeing the fear on his stupid face, knowing you had power over him? I bet it felt good. I bet you got a boner."

"I'm hanging up now, Martin."

"And you copped a five-day suspension. Bit rough, that. Sort of ironic too. You go for, what, years having the shit kicked out of you and nothing happens to your tormentors. Am I right?"

"Correct."

"And now you finally fight back and what happens? You get caught and punished. I tell you, it's enough to destroy your faith in the entire justice system."

"Life isn't fair, Martin."

"Exactly my point. You're learning, my fat friend. You're learning. So why don't we stop pretending? It's so much easier when you give up all those illusions and realize that the only justice you'll get in this life is the justice you dish out. It's a dog-eat-dog world out there, mate. You need to sharpen your teeth. Don't get angry. Get even."

"Goodbye, Martin."

I hung up.

I was in bed by ten o'clock. The storm had eased, but there were still occasional flashes of lightning that flickered white across my room. The thunder was a distant and occasional rumble. I needed to sleep. It was cooler now. The rain had washed some of the heat away. I pulled the blanket up to my neck.

Mary had been excited after Leah left. She kept darting glances at me, but she didn't say much about Leah. It was like she worried that talking would cause everything to disappear. Like a dream. So she gabbled on, chain-smoking and wrestling with my costume.

I couldn't work out what it was supposed to be. She had layers of material spread out and was busy on the sewing machine, but the costume was a shapeless mess. I didn't ask. I didn't want to burst her bubble. I sat opposite and half listened to the flow of words. It was a peaceful time and I wanted to enjoy it.

The image of Mary, happier than I'd ever seen her, enfolded me like a blanket. At the first signals of approaching sleep, my mind distanced itself from everything around. The flashes of lightning became pulses in my blood, drifting white into another world.

I stood at Leah's bedside. She held a battered teddy bear in her arms, hugged close to her body. I was glad I'd said I'd take her with me. Even though I'd have to describe it all to her in the morning. Well, some of it. I looked over my shoulder, and Leah was standing at the foot of her bed, watching herself sleep. She turned her eyes on me.

"Peaceful, aren't I?" she said.

"You're beautiful," I said.

I took her by the hand and led her outside. The night was dark and still. Overhead, clouds drifted apart and the moon gazed down on us. A dusting of stars appeared. An owl cried. We walked in silence. I wasn't in the mood for anything dramatic. I wanted to enjoy the peace. We went to a park. Leah showed me the way. The grass had been recently cut, and the air was full of its scent. There was a bench by a lake. We sat and watched the moon's reflection in the water, the way it shuddered when the surface was disturbed by a fish or an insect. I took her hand in mine again and raised her fingers to my lips.

"I have something to do," I said.

"I understand," she replied. "Don't be long."

"Stay here. I'll be back before you know it."

"I'll always be here for you, Michael," she said.

Jamie Archer's house was exactly as I had expected. The garden was overgrown, and the fly screens were ripped. Paint was peeling on the window frames. A dog was sleeping on the porch. As I got closer, it jumped up on quivering haunches and bared its teeth. I raised my hand and it slumped back. The front gates were padlocked but I passed through them. It was a single-story house. I walked straight through the front door.

Inside the house there were dishes stacked high in the sink, and the kitchen smelled of cabbage and tomato sauce. Cockroaches scuttled across the draining board as I walked past. I moved along a dark corridor toward the bedrooms. I put my head through the first door on my right. A man and a woman were sleeping in a large bed. The man was snoring slightly, and the woman's arm was draped over the side of the bed. Her mouth was open, and a web of saliva joined her parted lips. The room smelled of tobacco and alcohol.

I moved to the next room.

Jamie was asleep, but his dreams were troubled. He twitched slightly and moaned, turned violently on his side as I moved toward him. He had ointment on his face. Something for acne, I supposed. It glistened in the moonlight. I sat on the edge of his bed.

The room was untidy and smelled of stale sweat. Clothes littered the floor. There were cobwebs in the corners of the ceiling. It was an unhappy room, a room where Jamie had done a lot of crying. And there was anger. The room was soaked in it. Jamie turned away from me in his sleep, and I saw the side of his face brailled in angry sores. A muscle in his neck jumped.

"Jamie," I said. I kept my voice low and gentle. "Jamie, is this any way to greet a guest?"

His right eye snapped open. He didn't look toward me. I

could feel his terror. It hung heavy in the air. He stared blindly at the wall, willing my voice to be an extension of his dreams. I waited until his muscles started to relax and I saw his eyelid droop toward closure.

"Jamie," I repeated. "Wakey-wakey."

He jolted upright in his bed. His eyes were filled with horror. I almost felt sorry for him. He stared at me and his lips were quivering. There were tears and terror in his eyes. His shoulders shook. When he spoke, his voice was strangled with tension. He tried to keep control and failed.

"What the fuck? You are in deep fuckin' shit, man. Deep shit. This is . . . This is fuckin' breakin' and enterin', man. You're in deep shit."

"Jamie." I put a reassuring hand on his shoulder, but he flinched from me and scuttled over to the other side of the bed, hyperventilating. He gathered the sheet up to his chest. Maybe it was just as well. I didn't want to touch that acne, but I needed him to calm down.

"Jamie," I said, my voice low. It was important that one of us kept control. "Listen to me. Breathe deeply and settle down."

He shuddered again, but his breathing slowed a little. I made no move to get closer.

"Listen," I said in the same soft tone of voice. "There are a couple of things you need to know. First, and most important, I am not in deep shit. You are, my friend. You are."

He tried a sneer, but the muscles in his face weren't working properly. It came out wrong.

"Oh yeah?" he said, gulping for the words. "If I yell, my dad'll be down here in about ten fuckin' seconds and he'll rip your fuckin' head off, you freak."

I spread my arms wide.

"Be my guest," I said. "Yell as loud as you can."

He tried. His mouth opened and he breathed deeply into his diaphragm. But nothing came out. I stopped the noise at his lips. I made the air into blotting paper that sucked up the sound. His face turned red.

"That's the second thing you need to understand," I said. "You can't do anything, Jamie. You are completely in my power. Do you remember what I said to you this afternoon, outside math? Do you, Jamie?"

His face was still red, and he continued his silent screaming, but his eyes told me he remembered.

"I said I would come for you. And I have." I laced my fingers in my lap. "I said I would rip your heart out, Jamie. I could do that." I looked into his face. He was trying to move. I knew he couldn't. I waited for him to realize that struggling was no good. It was important for him to be completely aware of the situation. A clock ticked at the side of his bed.

I wanted to get back to Leah. But it was vital not to rush this. It was necessary to take my time. I allowed a minute to go by.

"You see, Jamie," I said, "you have no idea what my life has been like, the suffering I've put up with. From you, Jamie. And people like you. I want to give you a taste. Consider this as a learning opportunity."

I settled myself more comfortably on his bed before continuing.

"How does it feel, Jamie? To be helpless and terrified? Do you know you've pissed yourself?" I pointed at the growing wet patch in the sheet. "Does it worry you that your terror will have absolutely no effect upon the outcome of this evening? In a decent world, I might have pity. But this isn't a decent world, Jamie. This is a world where the strong make the weak suffer. I've learned that from you."

I kept my eyes locked on his and saw they were filled with horror.

"I'm not going to kill you, Jamie." I paused and let the words sink home. "I'm not unreasonable. But you see, you're a symbol of all the crap I've ever been through. In every school. It's unfair that you have to pay for all the others. *I* know that. But it's not a fair world. *You* know that. I guess we'll both have to live with that unfairness."

I stood up and moved around the bed until I was standing above him. He couldn't move. Martin was right. This *was* fun.

"Tell me something, Jamie. Are you right-handed or left-handed?"

He gurgled but I couldn't make out the words.

"You'll have to speak more clearly, mate," I said. "I'll assume you're right-handed. The odds are better."

I reached down and took his left hand in mine.

"It's actually quite interesting, Jamie. Did you know the word *sinister* comes from the Latin for *left*? And *dexterous,* which means 'skillful,' is from the Latin for *right.* The left hand has always been associated with things that are evil."

I broke his little finger.

"The Catholic Church once proclaimed that all left-handed people were servants of the devil. Isn't that barbaric?"

I snapped his ring finger. That was difficult. I had to use more force.

"It wasn't long ago that left-handed kids were punished in school and forced to use their right hands for writing."

I'd gotten used to it by now. His other fingers were easy. I left his thumb intact. To be honest, I thought it was going to be difficult to break his thumb. And I'd made my point. I placed his ruined hand back in his lap.

"Isn't that interesting? Well, I think it is. Anyway, it's time for me to go. I'd love to stay and chat, but I've got things to do. Sleep well, Jamie."

But I thought it unlikely.

I sailed down the corridor toward the front door. There was no sound in the house except low snoring from the main bedroom.

The place was filthy. I felt sorry for Jamie. No one should have to live in that kind of mess.

Outside, the sky continued to clear. The moon was picked clean by the wind. I took fresh air into my lungs and allowed Jamie his voice back. I could hear his screams as I walked to the park. I sat beside Leah on the bench, and we watched the lake. I still had most of the night at my disposal.

"So. The hospital," I said.

Leah squeezed my hand.

"Let's start in the children's ward," she said.

That was fine by me. I knew it would make her happy.

Friday

1.

Dad left a note on the kitchen table. "Clean this crap up." I found it among the pieces of material, propped up on the sewing machine. There was no sign of Mary.

The kitchen door was open. It was ten in the morning. I'd thought I would wake at the normal time, but the previous evening must have taken it out of me. I sorted through the material. The costume was mostly on the floor. I shook it out but still couldn't tell what it was supposed to be. So I made toast and coffee. I'd tidy up later. I had the whole day ahead of me and nothing to do.

I took my breakfast into the garden. Wisps of cloud trailed

delicately over blue sky. The palm trees were refreshed, their leaves glistening green after the storm. Beads of rainwater, trapped in foliage, flashed when the sun's rays caught them. The air was clear and cool.

I found Mary by the pond in the corner of the garden. She was smoking and gazing out over the fence. She glanced up as I approached and she smiled, a timid thing that struggled to keep its shape. I put my arm round her shoulder. Her eyes were red and puffy.

"What's the matter, Mary?" I said.

She shuddered slightly and turned her head from me. There was silence. I wondered if she was going to answer.

"Oh, Michael," she said finally. And then she shook with sobs. It was as if the act of speaking pressed a switch and all of her emotions flooded out. She cried so hard, she couldn't get her breath. She gulped and howled.

"Mary, what is it?" I said. "You're scaring me." I tried to turn her head, but she wouldn't let me see her face.

"It's the costume." Her voice was broken. "It's a disaster, Michael. I can't get it right. I've been up half the night working on it, and no matter what I do, it's wrong." I hugged her but she got angry. "It's not even complicated." She thumped me on the arm as if it was my fault. "I'm bloody useless, that's all. A simple costume and I can't even get that right. I'm totally hopeless. A waste of time and space."

I couldn't help it. I laughed. She hit me on the arm again.

"And now it's funny, is it? All the work I've put in and you find it funny? Well, go on, have a good laugh. Stupid bloody Mary. Can't do a thing right."

I hugged her closer. She tried to resist. But not much.

"It doesn't matter," I said. "It's not important. I can rent a costume. It's nothing to get upset about."

She broke away from me, and her eyes were even angrier. I'd said the wrong thing.

"Nothing to get upset about? Of course it isn't. You think it's silly and trivial. I wanted to make your costume for you, to get it right. I wanted it to be good. So you could go to the Social with something of me. Something to be proud of. I'm stupid for thinking that might be important. Go rent a costume, Michael. That's what you should have done in the first place. We both knew I wasn't up to it. I'm useless."

I didn't know what to do. I'm no good at this sort of stuff.

"Mary, I'm sorry. I didn't mean that. I didn't want to upset you."

"No? And what did you mean to do? Go rent a costume. Leave me alone."

She went to move off, but I couldn't let it end like that. I stepped in front of her.

"I want you to make the costume, Mary. Please? I don't want to rent one. Honest."

"You're just saying that to make me feel better. A few moments ago you were all in favor of renting one."

"Yes, but I hadn't thought it through!"

"What do you mean?"

"I can't afford it. I don't have any money."

She froze. And then she laughed. She laughed as hard as she had cried before. I smiled. I didn't know how I had done it, but I'd won her over.

Mary felt better after a cup of tea. She sat at the table and drank it while I put most of the bits and pieces of material away. I stuffed them into a garbage bag. Finally, we were left with the costume. I shook it out.

"It's fine," I said.

"What is it, then?" said Mary.

"Can I phone a friend?"

That got her laughing again.

"Listen," I said. "I've got an idea. This is kind of . . . well, shapeless. No offense. So why don't we make it more shapeless? Add strips of material all over it. We've got plenty. Make it into a cloak of some kind, ragged, torn, and dirty. Add a hood."

Mary raised her eyebrows.

"Then," I continued, "I could smear dirt all over my face and go as someone who's risen from the grave. Or maybe one of those evil creatures from *Lord of the Rings*."

She kept her eyebrows raised.

"It won't matter which. I don't have to tell anyone. People can use their imagination. And the beauty of it is, it doesn't have to look like it's . . . professionally made." I kept an eye on the door in case I had to make a run for it.

There was a pause.

"Pass me the dressmaking scissors," said Mary.

My eyes snapped open. For a moment I couldn't place the noise. Then it came again. A knock at the front door.

I went to open it and my body felt fluid. Muscles moved like liquid beneath my skin. Nothing missed my senses, the feel of bare feet on cold floor, the way my hair ruffled slightly under the ceiling fan, the tingle of blood in my fingers. I felt charged.

Mr. Atkins seemed embarrassed. He stood on the porch as if he was sorry someone had answered. He was half turned toward the street. I got the feeling he was at the point of leaving. His smile, when he saw me, was nervous.

"Ah, Michael, my boy," he said. "Good to see you. Good to see you. Could you spare a few minutes? I wonder if I might have a quick word?"

"Of course, Mr. Atkins. Please come in."

"Is your father at home?"

"He's at work. But my stepmum should be back in a moment. She's just popped out to the shops."

Mary had run out of thread.

"Ah." Mr. Atkins seemed mildly surprised. "I didn't know you had a stepmum, Michael. We'll have to update our records. Very slack."

"Dad filled out my enrollment form. He must have forgotten to mention Mary."

Mr. Atkins blinked.

"I'm sorry, Mr. Atkins. Did you want to talk to her?"

"No. It was you I wanted to talk to. But I thought that maybe a parent or guardian should be present. You know."

"Well, she'll be back soon. In fact, she should have been here a while ago. Come in and wait, Mr. Atkins. I'll make you a cup of coffee."

He seemed reluctant. I stood back from the door and waited. Finally, he came in.

"Well, if you're sure she'll be back soon."

It was strange. Mr. Atkins was nervous and I was calm. He followed me into the kitchen and sat at the table. He put his briefcase on the floor.

I put the kettle on and spooned instant coffee into mugs.

"Milk? Sugar?" I asked.

"Black with sugar. Thanks."

"How many lumps?"

"Two, please."

When I'd fixed the drinks, I sat opposite and we sipped from scalding mugs. "Did you come to talk about my suspension, Mr. Atkins?" I said. I was curious.

He put his mug down and glanced around. I was glad I'd tidied up. It wasn't anything like his home, but it wasn't too bad. It was strange. I knew what his place looked like, and he didn't even know I'd been there. It gave me a feeling of power.

"Yes," he said. "Yes, about the incident yesterday. The fight between you and Jamie Archer."

He was becoming more nervous. He kept glancing at the kitchen door as if willing Mary to enter. A coin appeared in his right hand and wheeled across his knuckles. I got the impression he didn't even realize he was doing it.

"I feel . . . well, responsible is the word, I suppose."

"You shouldn't, sir. I did it."

"Yes, but it's not quite that simple. If I understand correctly, the fight came about because of remarks made about me."

He glanced at me but I didn't say anything.

"You were . . . defending my honor, I suppose. And that makes me a part of the matter. I cannot justify your actions, Michael. Violence doesn't solve anything, as I'm sure you know only too well. But, misguided though your response was, I wanted you to know I am grateful for the sentiments behind it."

"No problem, sir."

"No." Mr. Atkins put his hands flat on the table. There was no sign of the coin. "There is a problem. I want you to listen carefully, Michael. What you did was wrong. Homophobia is a fact of life in high school. It comes with the territory. Year Nine and Ten boys, in particular, seem obsessed with it. Personally, I believe it's a rite of passage." He was warming to his theme, and the coin appeared again, spinning across his fingers. "Statistically, I understand a significant number of the boys I teach will come to realize in later life that they are homosexual. I also know the path to that realization will be a painful, even tortured one. I cannot blame them for their attitudes now. They are children. It's unreasonable to expect them to behave as if they weren't. Do you understand me?"

"Yes, sir."

"I'm not suggesting homophobia in schools should be ignored. Don't get me wrong. You were right to speak up. But you were wrong to use violence as a way of enforcing your views. It's counterproductive. It legitimizes prejudice. If you find yourself in that situation again, I want you to walk away. Promise me, Michael."

I thought about it. I wasn't sure I agreed with him. Maybe Dad was partly right. If you wanted to make the world a better place, then sometimes you had to meet violence with violence. Sometimes it was the only way to bring about change.

"What if words aren't enough, sir?"

"They *have* to be enough, Michael." He was really serious. There was no laughter in his eyes. "Because if they aren't enough, we might as well forget it all. Forget justice, morality, and any sense of human decency. We cannot go down that path, Michael. It leads only to destruction."

I thought about wars. How sometimes, faced with evil, there is no choice but to fight back. Wasn't that what the Second World War was all about? My memory of the lessons on it was hazy. But wouldn't evil have won if no one had fought to stop it? Mr. Atkins would probably have an argument, but I didn't want to discuss it. He'd asked me to promise. It was important to him and would make him happy. It was easy to do. After all, it was only words.

"I promise, Mr. Atkins," I said.

"Good boy, good boy." The coin vanished and Mr. Atkins sprang to his feet. "I have to go," he said. "Your stepmum hasn't returned, and the lunch break at Millways is rapidly diminishing." He smiled. "Thank you, Michael."

"No worries, sir."

I showed him to the door, and he hurried down the path. I watched his back. He seemed vulnerable. But I would look after him. That made me feel better.

"Mr. Atkins?" I shouted.

He turned.

"Give my best wishes to your wife," I said.

His expression was puzzled. I couldn't blame him. He had no way of knowing I even knew she existed. As I closed the door, he was still staring at me. Mary returned a minute later.

2.

We finished the costume and it was impressive. And totally shapeless. Long strips of material trailed on the floor. The hood was like a sack. I had to keep pushing it back off my face. If Mary had been skilled on the sewing machine, it wouldn't have been so effective. I didn't tell her that, though. She was pleased. She tried to be all gruff and critical when I tried it on. She pulled at stray hems, pushed the material around. But I wasn't fooled. I could see pride in her eyes.

Mary insisted I try some makeup as well. She didn't have much in the way of cosmetics, so I went out to the front of the house and scraped up dirt from the garden. It was then I saw him. The boy. He was about a hundred meters down the road, talking into a mobile phone. I couldn't see his face. He was in the shade of a mango tree, and he had a baseball cap pulled low. He might not even have been watching my house. I knew, though. Something about the way he stood.

The dirt was effective, but it felt uncomfortable. I smeared it on with water, and when it dried, it flaked off. I found a marker and blacked out a couple of my teeth. That looked sinister but tasted foul. We decided it wouldn't matter. The costume was so baggy no one would see much of my face anyway. I showered and then made something to eat. There were still several hours to kill.

Leah rang and we arranged for her to come to my house so we could go to the Social together. Then I went to my bedroom. Even though I had slept late, I felt tired. Anyway, I didn't have anything to do. The house was tidy enough. I read my book for a while and then peered out the window. The boy was still there. He'd moved to another tree, but he was still there. I wondered how many hours he would keep watch. Then I drew the curtains and lay down on the bed. I stared at the ceiling and thought I wouldn't drift off. My eyes closed.

Mummy checks my seat belt again. She tugs on it, and the frayed strap breaks off in her hand. I play with a small truck in my lap. It is red, and there's a patch on the roof where the paint has been chipped off. If I pick at it, I can make more paint flake. The doors on it open and everything.

We drive. Mummy talks but I'm not listening to what she's saying. I keep opening the truck's doors. Close. Open. It's sunny. As we turn corners, the sun shines off the loose seat belt buckle in my lap. Dazzles me.

Then the sun is somewhere else. It goes flash, flash, flash. I feel sudden pain. Mummy's arm against my chest. She's hurting me. Pushing me back into the seat. I turn my head and her face is fixed straight ahead. There is something awful in her eyes, but I have no time to read it. Her mouth is turned down, and I can see muscles bunching in her bare leg. Her right leg is straight out in front of her. She is wearing shorts. They're blue and have a pattern around the edges. I turn my head. There is a loud noise. Her arm keeps pressing me back.

The world turns and keeps on turning. When it stops, there is pain in my leg and a nasty smell. I get to my feet. I'm crying for Mummy, but she's not there. There is grass all around, and my leg is scraped. Blood oozes down it. The toy truck is still in my hand. The car is against a tree. It's bent and twisted and makes a ticking sound. I go closer. One door is open. My door. My leg hurts and I can hear someone screaming from a long way away. I think it might be me. I look through the windshield. Mummy is there, but she's twisted as well. Her eyes are closed, and there is a thin trickle of red leaking out of the corner of her mouth. I call to her.

Then colors flood. I feel the sound. A searing *whumpf.* I'm picked up by the sound. It makes me fly. Everything goes dark.

• • •

Leah came to the house at five o'clock. Mary had insisted I be ready on time. I'd sat in the cloak for nearly an hour, sweating. I couldn't get grumpy, though. She was too happy for that.

Leah was going as a ghost. She had a huge white sheet with a couple of holes cut out for eyes. It was simple, but I could tell Mary was pleased. My costume was really cool in comparison.

We decided against traveling to the Social in our costumes, particularly since we'd be getting the bus. So we stowed them in my backpack. Mary was disappointed. She had been looking forward to waving us off, all dressed up. We overruled her.

We left the house. I watched out for the boy. He might have been there, somewhere, but I didn't see him.

3.

The day closed as it always does in the tropics. It slammed shut.

Leah and I approached the school. It was different somehow. Cloaked in darkness, most windows blank and unseeing. A place of shadows. Here and there, security lights cast a pale, weak glow. A few hundred meters away, we took the costumes from my backpack and put them on.

The hall was an oasis of light. Colored bulbs were strung along the front. Light leaked from shuttered windows. We heard voices from a long way off. A buzz of excitement and other emotions mingled in a thin whine. The thump of bass swirled in with the surrounding noise and lost its form, like milk in coffee.

Cars entered and exited the car park as students were

dropped off. A small knot gathered outside the hall. A bat, startled by our approach, was a smudge of darkness against the sky. It flew into the night with a rasp of leather wings. The lights drew us. My cloak trailed behind me. I had the hood up and it framed the hall. Leah held my hand.

There was a long trestle table at the entrance. Senior students were behind it, selling drinks and potato chips. A sign announced a sausage sizzle, starting at seven-thirty. A girl in a devil outfit was tending a barbecue, scraping metal over the surface. The smell of onions tickled my nose, and my stomach turned with nervous hunger.

I handed my ticket to a teacher I didn't know. She seemed irritable, as if this was an annoying duty. As Leah and I went inside, she glanced at her watch.

Noise washed over us. The bass was like the thump of the building's heartbeat. A young guy was bent over a machine with dials and knobs. Two huge speakers squatted on each side of the stage. The front of the machine was a panel of colored lights, blinking in time to the music. A handful of students were washed in a sequence of changing colors.

The stage was fringed with a long banner. "Welcome to Millways High Year 10 Social." The edges of the fabric had been trimmed with various designs. Bats. Witches' hats. Two glowing, life-size skeletons were suspended over the speakers. A cigarette was clamped between the teeth of one.

The main area of the hall had been divided into sections.

Nearest to us was a cave made from black resin. A glow of candles lit it from the inside. A couple of shapes moved within the textured darkness. Another area featured a graveyard, with headstones. Students were using them as seats. A few coffins, lids open, were interspersed among the graves. Another section was designed as an Egyptian tomb. The painted backdrops rippled slightly in the air-conditioning, giving the illustrated stonework a strange, unearthly effect. Gold hieroglyphics flashed reflected light.

The area in front of the stage had been kept clear for dancing. A few girls danced in a circle, shutting out everyone else. The rest of the space was a maze of dark recesses. The ceiling was studded with black balloons.

Leah and I stood for a few moments, absorbing the atmosphere. I hadn't expected something on this scale. Students flowed through the doors in a steady stream. Nearly all were in costume. Vampires, mummies, monsters of all kinds. They shrieked with pleasure as they recognized each other. They hugged and laughed. Excitement filled the air like a drug. Leah and I wandered over to the far wall, which was lined with benches. A few students sat, chatting. We found a quiet space. I pulled my hood down.

"I can't see them," said Leah.

"Who?"

"Martin Leechy or Jamie Archer."

"I don't think Jamie will be making it," I said.

"Why not?"

"Just a feeling."

Leah went outside to get drinks. I watched the gathering crowd. I didn't even see Mr. Atkins approaching. He sat next to me before I was aware of it.

"Well, Michael," he said. "You look . . . How can I put it? Positively evil. That's a brilliant costume, my boy. Simple, yet evocative."

"Thanks, sir."

"And what do you think of the hall, eh? Something of a transformation, wouldn't you say?"

"It's cool, sir."

Mr. Atkins sat back on the bench and sighed, as if it were all his own work.

"I tell you, Michael. This school has its faults. But at times like this I feel a paternal frisson for the place. It's even better than last year, and that was considered a tour de force among the cognoscenti."

I didn't know what he was talking about, so I said nothing.

Mr. Atkins reached out, as if he was going to touch me on the arm. Then he seemed to think better of it. He locked his fingers together.

"I'm very glad to see you here, Michael," he said. "Very glad indeed. I didn't think . . . Well, never mind what I thought. I hope you will use this evening to make contact. Talk to other students. Get the trick of it." He pulled out a coin and made it vanish again. "Remember?"

A smile played around my lips, but it soon faded. Far off in the corner of the hall was a boy who wasn't in costume. He had a baseball cap pulled low, and he was talking on a mobile phone. His eyes were in shadows. It was too far away to see clearly, but I knew he was staring at me as he talked.

"I have to go, Mr. Atkins," I said.

"By all means, Michael. Mingle, my boy. As E. M. Forster would undoubtedly say: only connect."

And I did. I made the connections. Jamie Archer had friends, many of them. Was the boy in the cap one of the ones outside Mr. Williams's math class? I couldn't be sure. Not unless I saw his face clearly. But I was nearly certain.

I did know I was safe in here. I could sit next to Mr. Atkins or stand by the teacher at the door. Probably even arrange a lift home. But Leah was out there somewhere. Getting drinks for us. She had been a long time. Too long. I stood.

I made my way to the exit. The crowds parted to let me pass. I couldn't see the boy in the red cap now. He had disappeared into shadows. A student stamped the back of my hand so I could get back in again. Gentle rain was falling, a fine mist dancing in the lights. Miss Palmer was at the door now, laughing with a group of students. She smiled at me and waved. I didn't wave back.

The trestle table was under cover, and there were dozens of students buying drinks. Farther along the wall, the barbecue was smoking, a cloud of shimmering heat rising. The smell of sausages and onions drifted and tantalized. A larger crowd was gathered there, maybe four deep. Some were jostling, shouting over the heads of those in front. I couldn't see Leah. I walked slowly past both lines, just to make sure. Perhaps she had gone back inside. Maybe she was wandering the hall, trying to find me.

I didn't think so.

I walked around the corner of the hall and followed the wall toward the oval. The sounds of the Social were muffled here, though the wall on my left pulsed with energy. Suddenly the world was empty. Scores of students were a few meters away, but I felt completely alone. I kept walking to the end of the hall wall.

The oval was a black curtain. I could see faint outlines of trees against the sky. A moonless night. The rain pressed in and I put my hood up. Nothing moved within the darkness. I turned left along the back of the hall. I had a strong sense of being watched. It was a pressure between my shoulder blades. Once or twice I turned, certain someone was a few paces behind me. Each time no one was there.

When I reached the far corner, I heard a dim buzz of conversation. I was in front of a classroom used by the Phys. Ed. staff. It jutted near the edge of the oval. I moved slowly, stretching my neck to peer around the corner.

For a moment I could see nothing. Then three tiny spheres of red light came into focus. They swayed lazily in the dark. The murmurs came from behind the glowing balls. I took a step forward and the voices stopped. The lights danced crazily, then disappeared.

"Who's there?" The voice was brittle with anxiety.

I stepped forward again. Even with my eyes adjusted to the night, it was difficult to see the three boys. They were hunched together against the wall, hands behind their backs. When they saw me, they relaxed. I wasn't a teacher. One boy moved out of the shadows. He pointed at the cowl of my cloak.

"Who are you?" he said. "I can't see your face."

I lowered the hood. He squinted into my face and turned to his friends.

"It's all right," he said. "It's that fat bastard. The new kid."

They took lighted cigarettes from behind their backs and drew hungrily on them. The tips glowed brightly, staining their lips and fingers red. They ignored me.

"Christ. Thought it was a teacher for a moment."

"Yeah, you shat yourself, Darren."

"Did not."

"Did too."

"I'm looking for a girl," I said. They shut up then, but only briefly. Then they cracked up laughing. Their giggles were shrill at the edges.

"Aren't we all, mate?" said one of the boys. It might have been Darren. "Mind you, she'd have to be pretty desperate to be with you." The other two almost choked with laughter. They bent over, gasping for breath. The boy smiled, proud of his wit. I took another step.

"Shut up," I yelled. "Shut up and listen."

They did. Before their shock could dissolve to anger, I described Leah. I told them she might have been with a boy or boys. I said she wouldn't be with them willingly. The boy who'd spoken first was the quickest to recover. He took a step toward me. His lips were twisted into a snarl. A bead of spit pooled at the corner of his mouth.

"Nah," he said. "We haven't seen anyone, ya fat shit." He stuck a finger in my face. "And who do you think you are, talking to me like that? You're asking for it—"

I grabbed his finger and twisted. Surprise flooded his eyes and then pain. I increased the pressure. His knees buckled and he crouched in front of me. The other two boys jerked forward, but I held up my other hand and stopped them. I reached down and took the boy's lighted cigarette. Very slowly I closed my fist over it. The smell of burned flesh lingered in the air. I let the boy go and placed the crushed cigarette into his palm. There was fear in his eyes, but I had no time to pay attention.

"Thanks for your help," I said.

I pulled my hood up and pushed past them. The two boys

pressed themselves against the wall to let me through. I turned the corner of the building. The darkness of the main school towered in front of me. Nothing moved but I could feel eyes watching. I walked away from the hall and entered the shadows draping the school.

4.

The sounds of the hall were faint. Emptiness and darkness surrounded me. My footsteps echoed on the paths. Occasionally I heard the skitter of animals. A few times, slight movement at the corner of my vision made my head snap around. Shadows played tricks. More than once I thought I saw a figure hunched in a dark recess. My heart pounded but there was nothing there.

The school was a network of stairs and walkways snaking along the outside walls. Guardrails, as high as my shoulder, stopped anyone from falling. On a hunch, I took the first set of stairs I came to. I found myself on a walkway that ran past C Block. Directly ahead, another flight of stairs led up to D Block.

Yellow security lights glowed above the stairs. The sense of being watched grew stronger. I knew someone was up there, tracking me. I stopped and craned my neck. The latticework of walkways and rails stretched toward the blackness of the sky. Plenty of places to hide. I watched for shifting shapes within shadows but couldn't see anything. I took another step forward.

I'm not sure if it was the movement or the noise that alerted me first. I caught a scuttling flash of movement down to my right. At the same time there was a cry of "There!" I took a half-step toward the railings and glanced down. A boy was running from the hall, his arm outstretched, one finger pointing toward me. Then more kids emerged from the shadows. Two, three, four boys converging on the staircase. I couldn't make out their faces. One had a red baseball cap. Another had red hair.

I glanced along the walkway. I had no time to get back to the stairs, let alone down them, before they'd be streaming up. I cursed myself for coming here, a place where there was nowhere to run. I looked up again. It was the only place to go, and I had wasted enough time. Already I could hear the pounding of feet on metal stairs. I pushed my hood down and ran toward the flight of stairs leading up to D Block.

Even as I raced up the stairs I knew my choices were limited. Face them or get off the building. They were faster than me—outrunning them wasn't an option. There were doors leading off the walkways into classrooms, but they would probably be locked. There wasn't even time to check. As I ran, I glanced around to see if I could double back. Each level had two sets of stairs, one at each end. If they followed my exact path, maybe I could get to the level I had just left and from there to the ground. But they had split up. Two were racing along C Block, below and slightly behind me. The others had reached the bottom of the stairs I had just taken. They were covering all exits. Driving me upward.

Sweat was pouring off me, dripping into my eyes, making them sting. My vision was blurred. There was no more shouting, just the clang of shoes on metal and the harsh sound of my own breathing. I got to E Block, but my legs were heavy, muscles binding and locking. I couldn't keep this up for much longer. I had to make a decision.

I made it to the end of the walkway and stopped. The running feet behind me were getting closer. They were on the same level, halfway along. Jamie Archer was leading. I could see the set of his jaw, fists pumping up and down as he sprinted toward me. No time to think.

I climbed up the metal bars of the guardrail, next to the stairs. There were four bars. I stood on the top and steadied myself with my left hand against the stair rail. I stooped to keep my balance, swaying slightly as I centered my feet. The bar was hard and narrow under my shoes. There was only blackness beneath and a dizzying drop. Slowly I raised my head. Only seconds remained. The clatter of running feet behind me was loud. I could sense Jamie reaching out for me as I bent, took a deep breath, and pushed away from the bar, sailing up and out into the darkness.

My hands grabbed the edge of the concrete ledge and clung on as my body pounded into the wall. It felt like a giant hand had slammed into my stomach, punching the air out. I closed my eyes as a wave of nausea spread through me.

The gap between the buildings was not great. Less than two meters, probably. But I hadn't been able to take a run up. It was a standing jump, and the roof of the other building was slightly above my head. Perhaps the adrenaline helped. Now I hung by my fingers down the wall face. Jamie could almost touch me. Almost. I could hear him and the others behind me. Maybe they were willing me to fall. Maybe they were stunned by what I'd done. But there was no shouting, no insults. All I could hear was a faint rush of air, their panting breaths, and my own heartbeat.

My arms started to ache. I tried to pull myself up before the pain robbed my muscles of strength. I opened my eyes and saw only the blur of gray concrete. My feet scrabbled at the wall but couldn't find any grip. If I could hook an elbow over the para-pet, I'd have a chance. But my body was a dead weight. I could feel the veins on my neck stand out. My face was slick with sweat and my hands were clammy. I held my breath and strained upward, willing the muscles of my arms to one final effort. For one brief moment, I thought I'd made it. My right elbow scraped the top of the wall. I was millimeters from hooking it over when my arms collapsed. One moment they were bunched, the next I was at full stretch again. But this time I had nothing left. My fingers, slippery with sweat, were losing their grip. I was seconds from falling, with no strength to do anything about it.

I've read that when you are about to die, you feel calm and peaceful. That didn't happen. All I felt was a surge of panic that bloomed and filled me. I couldn't scream. I couldn't breathe. There was no room for anything other than the rush of adrenaline. My mind focused on slick fingers and their slow slide. I felt no pain. Not then. A hard knot of determination kept fingers locked and everything else at bay. Time was almost frozen. Small frames that passed with painful slowness.

The hands gripped my wrists, just as my fingers loosened. Maybe I had a second or two left, maybe as many as ten. Impossible to tell. I felt the hands, cool and hard, and suddenly that dark force of gravity weakened. I pushed my feet against the side of the wall, and they found traction. My left elbow locked over the parapet, then my right. Hands grabbed the neck of my cloak. I was hauled up and over and onto the flat, safe surface of the roof. My breathing started again. I was tearing at the air, forcing great gulps into my lungs. My fingers were cramped and knotted.

It took me a few minutes to recover enough to get to my feet. Martin was standing there. He was smiling and shaking his head.

"Call yourself a Dreamrider?" he said. "You've got no idea, mate. No idea at all."

I flexed my fingers. Feeling was returning. I could tell from the pain. My arms hung limply. I stared at Martin. He didn't have a hair out of place. My breathing showed no signs of slowing.

"And what was that performance with Jamie?" he continued. "Breaking the fingers on his left hand? His *left* hand? Well, top marks for stupidity, mate. I mean, cool. I give you that. 'Sinister.' That was a nice touch. But you've got to learn, Michael. No pity. Because pity results in situations like this. Jamie has a good hand. Now he's going to use it. And do you think he'll take pity on you? You blew it, mate."

I couldn't think. His voice washed over me. Somewhere deep down, I knew what his words meant. But I wasn't ready to face that. Not quite yet. I pushed myself up straight and flexed my arms. I felt weak.

"Good thing I'm here to teach you," said Martin. "I told you. I told you I'd be here to help you. We're almost there, Michael."

"Where's Leah?" I croaked. "If you've hurt her . . ."

"Oh, for God's sake," said Martin. He snapped the words out. "I wouldn't hurt Leah. She's a part of me as much as a part of you. She's safe, okay? Now, if you've had enough of a rest, I think it's wise to move on. There's company on its way and it's not friendly."

He pointed behind me and I turned. Jamie and the others had left the walkway. They were roaming the stairs, scattered around the building. Searching for a way across. I knew that it was only a matter of time before they found it.

I ran across the metal sheeting of the roof. Martin was ahead of me, and I tried to keep up with him. But my legs were tired, my lungs straining, and the gap between us widened. I couldn't work out where we were. I was confused and the darkness was profound, the sky heavy with clouds. Rain spun into my eyes. Martin became a moving silhouette, a darker wedge against a black backdrop. My muscles were burning again, but I kept my legs moving.

I didn't see the wall until I was right up against it. I locked my feet against the slick surface of the roof and planted my hands in front of me as it loomed up. Even so, it was a painful blow when I collided with it. Exhaustion flooded through me. I leaned against the wall, head bowed, muscles twitching. Over the sound of my own gasping I heard the drum of urgent footsteps. Getting closer. I forced myself away from the wall and moved along the roof, to my right. There was no sign of Martin now.

I wasn't prepared for the lights. I turned a corner and there was another roof below me. It was ablaze. I stood for a few seconds, blinking, before I realized it wasn't fire. The roof of the hall. The Social. I heard excited voices, the familiar thud of the bass. Colored lights shone along the wall below me, to my right. Three or four skylights glowed with pulses of light at evenly spaced intervals in the dark expanse of corrugated iron.

The drop to the hall roof was about two meters. I had nowhere else to go. I could hear footsteps closing. I stepped up onto the narrow ledge and jumped. When the metal sheeting hit me, pain shot through my left leg. I fell heavily to the side, scrambled to my feet, and limped away. The noise was louder here. The roof vibrated to the music and the yells of students. I passed one of the skylights and peered down. It was a twenty-meter drop. I was above the stage area. The DJ was bent over his machine. The number of dancers had swelled now. A sea of heads swayed.

I passed two more skylights. This time I didn't look down. My gaze was fixed on the last skylight. It seemed important to get there. My progress had slowed, the pain in my leg getting worse. Wherever I looked there was only roof. No stairs, no exit. Nowhere to hide. Five meters short of the last skylight, I stopped. Above the noise of the Social I heard the clatter of feet landing on metal. I turned.

The boys were at the far end of the roof, fifty or sixty meters away. Jamie Archer was in the center. The other boys fanned out to the right and left. They walked slowly toward me. I backed away, my feet inching across the roof. I kept my eyes locked on the semicircle of approaching boys. Only when I scuffed up against the frame of the skylight did I stop.

I felt hands take mine. I glanced quickly to each side. Martin was on my left, Leah on my right. We stood there and watched Jamie and his mates close in. They were forty meters away now. Jamie was smug, lazily confident.

"You're dead, Terny," he said, and his voice, though soft, carried.

5.

Forty meters.

"You made us in your own image, Michael," said Leah. "And we're here to help you."

Martin chuckled.

"Bit of a Scrabble buff, eh, Michael?" he said. "Move those tiles around and *Michael Terny* becomes *Leah McIntyre, Martin Leechy.* Like magic. I reckon I got the worst deal, though. Leechy? Something that clings and sucks and has no backbone? You've got to admit, mate, that isn't me. But I guess there's only so many variants you can make out of the letters of your name. I forgive you."

Jamie was in no hurry. He knew, as I did, that there was nowhere for me to go. Beyond the last skylight was another ten meters of roof and then a high, featureless wall. He strolled, arms swinging gently. I tried to focus on his left hand, but it was lost in shadows. He kept his eyes fixed on mine.

"You never mention your stepmum's last name." Martin's voice was calm, controlled. No sense of urgency. "Mary what, Michael? I don't have your skill at anagrams, but here's an educated guess. Cheltine? Enelitch? Enelitch sounds Eastern European. Not that it matters, of course. Three of us. Born of your hopes and fears. Quite a feat, Michael. Keeping the three of us close, satisfying your needs. What a trinity!"

"I don't need you, Martin," I said.

He laughed. "You're wrong. You need me most of all. I mean, Leah's a lovely girl. Gentle, kind. But she's not a lot of help in this situation, is she? When things get nasty. 'Turn the other cheek, Michael.' 'Let's save the world, Michael.' And Mary's a sweetheart. I'd be the first to admit it. A sweet heart. But me, I'm your reality check. The others are good at touchy-feely. I'm the one who deals with boys with ice in their eyes and violence on their minds."

"Still talking to yourself, Wrenbury?" said Jamie.

Thirty meters.

I could feel the lip of the skylight against my heels. Leah gave my hand a firm squeeze but didn't say anything. Maybe Martin was right. I couldn't see how she could help me now. But it felt good to know she was there. Martin's grip was firmer. He was hurting my hand.

"I said I was going to show you. Here, at the Social." Martin's voice held no hint of anxiety. "The Dream. That's the key. Power. How to wield it, not just when you're asleep, but all the time. All the time, Michael. And you were so close. That idea about the Möbius strip. Twisting the two planes so they connect. That was good. Clever."

Twenty meters.

"But you haven't got the trick yet, have you? To travel between those two worlds whenever you feel like it. Yet the solution's been staring you in the face all this time. Literally staring you in the face. Do you know what I'm talking about?"

"No," I said.

"I think you do. I *know* you do. How could I know if you don't? The problem is, you've buried it, Michael. It's time to do some digging."

Ten meters.

"You're a crazy bastard, Wrenbury."

"Look behind you, Michael. Look down."

I did. The glass filled my vision. Framed by a metal edge, the glass was dark, but shapes were moving deep beneath the surface. The beat of the bass was like a distant ticking. Colors bloomed gently at the edges. Martin's voice seemed to come from a very long way away.

"What did you call it, Michael? A gateway from the Dream to the real world. But you didn't step through it. You watched. Just like you watched when your mother died. You didn't have the guts then, and you've never had the guts since."

A flash of yellow bathed the corner of the glass and then a seed of red. I knew what would happen. The colors would explode, fill the glass. And just before they did, I'd see what was there, beneath the surface. Any moment now. I tore my eyes from the glass, looked over my shoulder.

Five meters.

Martin's voice continued. Goading, pricking me toward that final twist of greatness. "But when you're through, the planes connect. The loop complete. Fixed. And who knows? This time you could stop the flames. Maybe your mother doesn't have to die. The Dreamride, Michael. Forever. Where you can make the world as you want it."

The colors grew. It was slow at first. It's always slow at first. Then they mushroom, explode. Jamie's arm was slow too. His fist traced an arc through the air, slicing the night. And then down. Picking up speed. Mushrooming speed. I ducked, came up under the slice of the punch. I grabbed Jamie, hugged him like a lover, my arms locked against his back, my face close to his. I didn't need to turn. His movement took us. I felt my feet leave the floor and then the glass giving, the explosion of noise and color, bathing us in fire.

We fell, like angels.

I made that final twist. Jamie's face was beneath me. I could see his eyes. There was no fear in them. Just deep bewilderment. Then the crack as we hit, the crash of a collapsing cave. And another crack, not loud, but final. We lay on the floor, me and him. No other sounds. His face was pale and freckled. His acne stood out like sparks, his neck twisted at a strange angle beneath the fire of his hair. There was nothing in the eyes now.

As I kissed him gently on the cheek, the pain bloomed within me. Along my arm and leg. It took away the light.

Saturday

There is something wrong with the light.

I focus on the people who float around me. Some have names attached to them. Others don't. There are people in white. They drift in and out. They control the pain. Making it worse and, once or twice, getting it to fade. Not entirely. I hug the pain to me. I see again the glass and the colors. I can't remember what it means. Faces appear sometimes. They swim into vision. I can see their eyes. Most times, there is nothing in them except curiosity. No emotion. It gets dark for a while.

There are faces from a long time ago. I remember. Mr. Atkins. His mouth moves, but if there is any sound, it is sucked up before it reaches me. My arm and my leg are still, and the pain has nearly gone. And so is Mr. Atkins. He is there one moment. I see the whiteness of the ceiling framing his face. Then he's gone. Like a vanishing trick. Instead there is a stain on the ceiling. Its shape resembles a map of Australia. I stare at it. I have something important to do, but I can't remember what it is.

Miss Palmer is there. She has a kind face. I can't hear what she is saying, but I listen to her eyes. There used to be fear there. I remember. Fear of me. Now I don't know exactly. It might be pity. The stain returns and is replaced by Dad. I watch his face. His nose has a grid of broken veins. Like the maps we used to draw of river systems in a school a long time ago. His breath is sour and there's fear in his eyes. I can't mistake that. It makes me feel good to know he's scared of me. He should be. He should be. But I don't know why.

It's quiet now. And dark. I can't see the stain. I'm lying in a bed but I can't move my head. There are straps over my legs and chest. I feel them as a dark pressure. If I swivel my eyes as far as I can, I see a metal rail on each side of me. Just enough light for that, but no more. I'm tied down. Locked in. My body can't move. Not yet. But they can't tie my mind down. They can't lock that in. Memories are coming back to me.

• • •

It's almost completely dark now. I can't even see the ceiling. But I hear. I can hear fine. And I can think fine. Mary is sitting at the foot of my bed. I know it's her. I don't need eyes for that. She doesn't say anything. Nothing at all. But she doesn't need to. I know she'll always be here for me. I feel that in the pressure at the end of the bed. No words needed.

An image sits behind my eyes. A strip of paper, twisted and joined. Stapled. In my mind I trace the journey over the plane. One plane now, where there used to be two. I go round and round. One to the other and there is no difference. I know what I can do. It's all clear now. I feel the power within me. Waiting to be released. Waiting for me to use it.

Martin is in the darkness to my left. He talks. He talks constantly. He talks of pain and punishment. He paints a picture of a man in a bar. A man who has had too much to drink. His car keys are in his pocket. He decides to have one more drink before going home. Martin tells of him going out to a car park, swaying. He has difficulty getting his keys into the lock. He scratches paintwork. He sits in the driver's seat. The car smells of sweat, tobacco, and alcohol. He starts the engine. He doesn't notice the dark shape in the rear seat, rising up. He doesn't see it until he turns in his seat to reverse out. And then the horror begins.

Martin talks of a man in silk shorts in a sea of fluorescent light. He is moving on his toes, dancing. He is talking about movement and the power in the shoulder. He is smiling as he jabs out a left, ducks his head, weaves and bobs. The fat boy opposite doesn't move. He stands there, his gloves at his side. The boy will move soon. When he's ready. And the man doesn't understand. He doesn't understand the power in the shoulder. But he will. He will when the boy decides.

Leah is in the darkness off to my right. Her voice mingles with Martin's. They talk at the same time, but I can hear what each is saying. It is all clear. She talks of Mrs. Atkins, of cancers gone, of children in hospital wards, of horror and pain banished. She describes a boy moving through the world. He cuts through pain and suffering. He moves into darkness and leaves behind him light. There are smiles on faces that were twisted with hurt.

I listen to their voices. They argue. They tell me what I should do. But I have my own mind. And there is room in that mind for both their voices.

I know what I will do. I know when I will start to do it. I will rest tomorrow. I am tired, because of everything I've done, everything I've created. But the day after tomorrow I will move within my world. And those who are good and pure of heart need fear me not. I will bestow on them all blessings. I shall take away their pain. Their suffering shall be as if it never was. And where there is darkness I will bring light, where there is fear I will bring hope, and my name will be praised above all others. Yet those who dwell in evil, who have not purity in their hearts, will tremble as I pass. I shall bring vengeance upon them, and their sufferings will endure forever. I shall cast out their evil, and the world will be born, new and afresh. And I will do this in my name. Michael Terny.

Because I *can* do this now. I can do everything.

To prove it, I lean forward into the darkness.

"Let there be light," I say.

And there is light.

Author's Note

Lucid dreaming is a "real" phenomenon, with many practitioners throughout the world. For those interested in learning how it can be done, any Internet search engine will provide many fascinating sites.

Unfortunately, in Australia and throughout the world, bullying in schools and mental illness among young people are also very real. Information and confidential help are available in all schools. There are also a number of very good Web sites that provide information and support.

On the issue of bullying, some good sources are:

www.nobully.com

www.lfcc.on.ca/bully.htm

www.kidshealth.org/kid/feeling/emotion/bullies.html

For help with matters of mental health:

www.kidshealth.org/teen/your_mind

www.focusas.com (Focus Adolescent Services)

Acknowledgments

Many people read early drafts of *Dreamrider* and provided invaluable suggestions. I would like to thank, in particular, Barb Clarke, Lauren Moss, Brendan Moss, Penni Russon, and Erica Wagner for helping to shape the final manuscript. I am doubly fortunate to have worked with two wonderful editors—Jodie Webster in Australia and Nancy Siscoe in the USA. Their enthusiasm and dedication have been more inspirational than I can adequately express. Thanks also to Angela Namoi, responsible for spreading my writing about the world, who said she was "smacked around" by the book. I hope that is a good thing.

To all my family and friends—thanks for your support and belief.

Saving the best till last: my wife, Nita, who makes me write when I don't want to, who always spots the flaws and tells me, who gives me space, support, and belief . . . thanks is too small a word.

About the Author

Barry Jonsberg was born in Liverpool, England, and now lives and works in Darwin, Australia. As a student, he was so desperate to avoid work that he stowed away in a university department for years, eventually emerging into the real world, blinking and pale, with two degrees in English literature.

His first book, *The Crimes and Punishments of Miss Payne,* was short-listed for the Children's Book Council Book of the Year Awards in Australia.

Barry is a supporter of Liverpool FC and, after the 2005 Champions League final, believes firmly in miracles. He also enjoys watching cricket and is still on a high after England's historic Ashes victory over Australia in 2005.